AUTOBIOGRAPHY OF CHILDHOOD

SINA QUEYRAS

Coach House Books | Toronto

first edition

 Canada Council   Conseil des Arts   ONTARIO ARTS COUNCIL   Canadä
for the Arts   du Canada   CONSEIL DES ARTS DE L'ONTARIO

Published with the generous assistance of the Canada Council for
the Arts and the Ontario Arts Council. Coach House Books also
acknowledges the support of the Government of Canada through
the Canada Book Fund and the Government of Ontario through
the Ontario Book Publishing Tax Credit.

This is a work of fiction. Any resemblance to any persons living
or dead is purely coincidental.

LIBRARY AND ARCHIVES CANADA CATALOGUING IN PUBLICATION

Queyras, Sina [date]
   Autobiography of childhood / Sina Queyras.
ISBN 978-1-55245-252-3
   I. Title.
PS8583.U3414A78 2011   C813'.6   C2011-904942-2

Autobiography of Childhood is also available in ebook format:
ISBN 978 1 77056 291 2

For a book-club guide to this and other Coach House titles,
please visit www.chbooks.com/bookclubs

for my family

'One day, I was already old ... '
– Marguerite Duras

She became aware of her own childhood one night in the middle of a very steep stairway. Caught halfway down, or up, she stares at the window in front of her and her childhood stares back, a smudge, perhaps already a stain, the edges of which she will spend a lifetime trying to discern. Later she might think there is something in coming to terms with oneself this way, children staring down through a banister at the light, puzzling the noise, finality versus eternity echoing in their heads. Trauma burns forever in the child's brain. But what is the trauma? Eternity? Finality? What comes first, the awareness of childhood or the awareness of death?

Unexpected, death is always trauma.

Yet there it lies, in the straggle of her childhood, death: completely insensible and ill-timed, a boa constrictor sprawled across the lap of the house, and now her father standing in the fast-food glow, tummy just beginning to protrude over his green work pants, salt-and-pepper strands falling like feathers over his brow. He is light on his feet, even with a paunch, and soft in the hands, despite the hard look of permanent grease stains. Five siblings huddle above on the landing, witnessing the monsoon of death in the A&W-coloured kitchen. She would like to tell you how he wept, describe his fingernails, curled like small insect wings, how he folded in on himself for a moment in the hallway below, how his physical shape created a space she is unable to fill ... but not now. Now she must look to objects. Now she must concentrate on the rooms in the house; the house that contains childhood; the kitchen that prepares the food of childhood; the food that is orange and watery, brown and runny, pale green, thick ketchup red. The room with cupboards that had been wood, that had once, her father argued just a few hours earlier, been beautiful.

But wood, however beautiful, isn't modern, her mother says, wood is depressing, so last-century, so impossible to clean, she would sooner pull the wooden cupboards down and leave them in the dust heap; she would sooner go without than have something drab, cracked, porous brown, wood, she said, ugh. She wants everything modern. Wipeable. Vinyl or plastic. So she starts with the cupboards. The orange insults his sensibility somehow; though even hip-high she knows that the idea of her father having a sensibility is ridiculous, even hip-high she suspects that he (and perhaps all fathers, maybe even all adults) is a puppet, that there is a line inside him below which nothing but impulse directs his movements. Her mother insinuated as much. Later she apologized for this, later she worried she had put her daughter off men. I love him, she said, that is why I can despise him.

She would like you to notice already how difficult it is to get at the story, how even without death, the thinking of one parent and another, the clash of wills, creates the tone of childhood. The back and forth of individual desire constructs the walls and doorways, the gates and stairways of childhood; the architecture of emotion, upright, solid as two-by-fours, stacked, ready for the swing of muscled arms and hammer blows. She would like you to notice how headlines and cutlines are also sashes and doorsills, how words float from print to tongue and back, or are whacked out of backyards with the force of aluminum bats, or caught in young, ungloved hands, small bones splintering unnoticed.

Stopped suddenly, childhood snags on years and is left dangling.

History is a great tree strung with the bright lights of childhood: now earthy, now grand, now Victorian, now plump, now ornate.

In this sapling childhood, things are complex. Outsides are patterned, but not yet branded. Corporations have not taken the idea of capital to its extreme, crafting each moment into product, amalgamating existing with consuming, thinking with advertising. In fact, there are still businessmen, sleek in felt hats and shiny shoes, who go home to mothballed closets and dreams of weekend golf, or boating, though inevitably end up at backyard barbecues, or legion halls playing shuffleboard and drinking squat bottles of Molson's.

In this childhood, the bright-coloured patterns clash. Furniture thickens and smooths, then becomes chiselled, limbs and hair lengthen and fray, seams soften, carpet grows to grass-like lengths, acid green, and is raked daily. Clothing becomes angular. Colours and patterns sharpen, become paisley, tart. People stand in line at the Dairy Queen. They are still under the illusion that they have choice. And perhaps some of them do.

There are no Nikes. No just doing anything. Her brother has black-and-white canvas runners in which he feels winged. There is no shock-absorbent sole, no microfleece lining. The eyeholes are metal, the laces so long they are double-knotted, the tips frayed. He runs around in the gym on days when the wind chill is too extreme, around the kitchen table before dinner, around his room at night, so fast no one sees him coming or going. He plans on running all the way to California where the curbs are flat, hydro poles buried underground and northern water piped down. The runners are not a specific brand; in fact, where the logo might be, a white plastic circle lies, an imaginative space. Empty, she knows, because she spends the morning of his death under his bed where they stare back at her like small creatures also awaiting his return.

(You understand that time is a skipping rope here, now twisted, now flattened, now enjoying double dutch? You understand that childhood is a flick of the wrist? Here is a gap. You can stand in it. Staring up. A beetle in a plastic cup. Go around and around. Something will come to you.)

She is going to tell you a story. He is going to tell you a story.

The story of childhood, of course, begins, with child-hood. This childhood. The one she is continuously experiencing, the one she never really left. It is not a famous childhood, not notorious or spectacular, you will not discover intellectual conversations occurring over macaroni and cheese, but it is nonetheless a story. Childhood is a story, always reconstructing as we remember. Tethered to the core of it, we are caught there; days spiral out and back in all weather. This is where the story begins, then. Here is a point of entry. Here, remember the shifting feet, the deafening newness of things, the absolute flounder of it. The sound of new. Remember how it rolled in your ears? Starting in the belly and rising in waves?

I could tell you a story, the twelve-year-old prostitute says. I could tell you a story, the young man selling pot on the corner says. Let me tell you a story, her coiffed students say in their neat rows. It begins like this ...

GUDDY

'It isn't good,' Helen says.

Guddy is perched on the arm of her red chair at the window, a favourite spot, from which she can take in much of her street. Her street, she recently discovered, was once home to the largest native population living off-reserve anywhere in North America. In the time of the Mohawks there was a bar around the corner called the TeePee. Many of the men who helped build the Manhattan skyline lived on her block. In fact, the apartment building on the corner was once occupied entirely by First Nations. They, like Guddy, left the village of the small huts to look for work, and probably like her were conflicted about going back, though as far as she could tell they had pretty much all left Brooklyn.

She listens to Helen, her sister's former partner and best caregiver, outline percentages, nursing details, snippets of conversation from the day. Rather, she tries to listen, to eke out the significant parts, to keep the many layers of her, and her sister's life, from boiling up and over into the street. The earliest glimmers of spring have arrived, not quite Vancouver's early spring, but in a way she thinks of New York and Vancouver as a matching set: New York does east coast the best, Vancouver does west coast the best. It's sunny in Vancouver, Helen tells her, though she knows that, she can always hear the weather in people's voices, it hits deeper notes, well beyond the surface disturbances of life.

'I'll come tonight,' she says, even as her head spins: she has classes to plan for tomorrow and Sara, her partner, due to fly out the next day, is managing several catastrophes, including the remnants of a sprained ankle.

'As soon as possible,' Helen says, sending a jolt up Guddy's spine, then, 'I'm sorry for the sudden turn.' Just yesterday Therese had said she would be home by week's end, and not to think of flying in.

'Does Therese know I'm coming? Can you tell her I'm coming?'

'Yes, she knows I'm calling you. She's sleeping now. They gave her something. It was a hard night.'

She puts down the phone, tentatively, each gesture now amplified, her thoughts as though they were leaving light trails in the air before her. She leans out the open window unsure whether she will lose her lunch or swallow air. An unexpected waft of soil from her empty flower boxes fills her nose and lungs. Someone – Mr. D, their landlord, most likely, has taken the robin's nest she had placed on the sill. He had been eyeing it all winter. Claimed to have never seen a bird's nest, and was unmoved by the perfectly cracked blue shells inside, remarking that he could not believe she would touch such a thing, never mind bring it all the way from Canada. He thought it might attract strange new forms of bugs, or vermin. The garbage, she reminded him, is where the vermin come from. Theirs is one of the last buildings on the street to deal with its sanitation situation, and the street-life rifles through it nightly.

She turns to find her partner, Sara, standing behind her, a bunch of cilantro dripping water on the egg cartons she has filled with soil, in preparation, overly eagerly as usual, to start her annuals.

'And?'

'My sister. It's time.'

'I'm so sorry.'

Sara extends her wet hands, but Guddy doesn't want to be held. 'We don't know anything,' she says.

'How long, you mean?' Sara comes at her again, and Guddy turns to the street.

'I just have to go.' Every summer of these past seven years has been the last, every Christmas the last, every spring the last, and now it may, finally, be the last, but even with all of this time for preparation she is not ready.

'Of course you do. When? Tomorrow?'

'Tonight if I can.'

'Would you like me to book for you?'

'No,' she says, 'I'll do it.' The neighbour's boys tumble from the brownstone down to the sidewalk. Brownstones, she has learned, are just brick covered in a mixture of concrete and brown clay. The next block down has been voted Greenest Block in Brooklyn three years in a row and her block would like to give them a run for their money, but they lack the organization and there are several large buildings that have nothing to do with street level – some kind of schoolboard office, where the employees gather outside to smoke at lunch, and a treatment centre that ensures a steady stream of colourful characters. Really, there is very little green on any Brooklyn street, but when the older trees reach out to each other they form a canopy, and when their tree wells are planted, it all creates a wash of colour and cool. The air really does seem different block to block.

Enough: she needs to book a plane ticket. She needs to dig out her Gore-Tex and warm socks. She should pack, email Gabe and Richard about drinks Friday night, cancel lunch with Avi, think about lessons, but what she does instead is stand at the window watching the firemen sweep the sidewalk around the memorial to the four men the station lost in 9/11. Every year on the anniversary, the company assembles in the street. Widows appear in grey or black. Sons are hoisted up onto the engine where they stand saluting as the men march, upright, faces sombre as flags. She has always had a soft spot for firemen. The orange of the career-counselling skill set, and despite the green of her own inquisitive nature, and the deep blue of her emotional creative core, she too has a large streak of orange, and really, it's the action that attracts her. Those who burst in through the flames and sweep babies from burning beds, those who do without thinking what it is that must be done.

And what has she done?

We are already so ineffectual, she sometimes complains to Sara, particularly after an evening with graduate students (love them, yes, but they are the most anxious, self-involved creatures on the planet). She doesn't mean it, of course, and Sara (herself a grad student) knows she doesn't mean it, but they can both appreciate the nugget of truth in it, the root-less academics, beholden only to their ideas. People who study literature, Sara argues, are in their way wanting to make a difference, if not by making a difference through their research and teaching, then at least by not taking part in the market. That's bullshit, Guddy argues, they're hiding away, not wanting to be part of the world. Wanting to go on about their own ideas with little or no regard for their impact or connection to the world, because they don't believe in the world.

The people Guddy ends up admiring are the ones who strap themselves to trees, who live off the grid (she has tried off-grid and failed), the people who go around the world mopping up after disasters (she has worked with youth in crisis and burned out), the people who physically make, or force, things to happen. Doctors Without Borders, Greenpeace, she envies them as she envies the firemen with their instant gratification. What a relief to have something concrete to do.

The boys across the street fall and roll up on their feet unscathed. They are not boisterous, they wear glasses, knock elbows, are more bookish than brawny, but with bounce. What makes one child thrive and another not? She is always watching children, trying to figure this out. Not that Manhat-tan babies in their nannied chariots are representative. Not the confident toddlers of Cobble and Boerum Hill, chewing on

Daddy's film treatment and kicking at Mommy's novel; running around in embroidered leather Prada shoes and drop-waisted organic cotton dresses. Beyond class, it's the swagger of accessibility, the confidence all New York kids gain by navigating the city, the sense of facility: all over the city, in the summer heat, the open hydrants, pubescent girls with garbage-can lids as shields waving sticks in the air.

She too had worn a cape, swung imaginary blades at rogues descending from mountaintops or scowling from coils of thickets that oozed danger at the edge of the little towns of her youth. As had Therese, though her sister was more like a great icebreaker ahead of the fleet: her tongue her sword.

Her sister Therese, lying now in her hospital bed, miraculously letting others make calls on her behalf, is equally orange, equally blue and green and stubborn in her pursuit of light and angle, of meaning. They were nowhere near culture growing up, nowhere near books or museums or galleries, and yet they both ended up in the thick of it. Therese was always unable to contain herself in any situation, out there on the edge of things, cataloguing the injustices, making art out of her life. Every corner of her world coiffed, the interior of her cupboards like a window display, bags of oatmeal plumped up for the camera, twist ties evenly placed and exactly twisted, stacked cans featuring bucolic, big-busted Italian women heaving baskets of tomatoes.

'My energy,' she had said the summer before, 'where has my beautiful energy gone?' And it was true. Her wide, Icelandic cheekbones were lost under the puff of progesterone. She was high on OxyContin, beaming like a pixie, landing like stone. The lack of energy was relative though: even battling cancer, Therese had more energy than most.

'Are you sure you don't want me to call? You're just sitting there.'

'No,' Guddy says, glancing at the clock, righting herself.

'Will you use your cell? And will you call now if you think you're going to get on a flight tonight? I have to keep the line free.'

Guddy nods, punches in the number off the back of her Aeroplan card. Of course she needs to call. Not calling isn't going to make it not happen. She needs to focus. She needs to not let herself drift, on top of everything else. She needs to be in this room. Now. This room and the room next to her where Sara waits for news. She had an interview in a city neither of them particularly wants to live in, though it is at a university and a department that Sara would be honoured to be part of. They have their own set of worries, which they were discussing just a few minutes ago and now suddenly have no more time to process. Perhaps that is what crisis does – it erases the past and the future, it makes the present all one need be concerned with.

After a surprisingly brief time on hold she is connected to a human voice. Sanjit, based in Vancouver, is unable to find a flight with Air Canada, but she has bought into Guddy's predicament and so has included her on a conference call with United, their Star Alliance partner, she keeps reminding her. They are mostly talking to each other as the United person sifts through flights out of the three available airports. Sanjit also has a sister with breast cancer and she is anxious herself. Health care is available to all in Canada but one still has to know how to navigate the system, find the best hospital, the best clinic, the best doctor for a given ailment: nothing is completely equal because neither human desire nor ability is equal. 'Who is your sister's oncologist?' They are both relieved that the doctor they perceive to be the best is the same woman.

She should be packing while waiting; she is always doing something when she is on the phone, a fact that bothers her sister. *Can you ever call just to talk to me?* Technically, when she is speaking on the phone she is talking to only one person, but she rarely does any one thing for its own sake, so there is the running of water, the swish of a broom, the sizzle of tofu or, if she is on her cell, shopping, walking, looking at art. She is a chronic multi-tasker, always trimming a minute here, maximizing a minute there. She has even worked her commute to New Jersey down to one hour and twenty-seven minutes. This includes arriving at Penn Station at 8:23 for an 8:29 train. It's touch and go if the train is on track 11, or if the A train gets stopped in the tunnel, but she cannot abide a twenty-minute wait staring dumbly up at the board.

Well, you have my attention now, she thinks.

Sara is preparing for a job talk, which for some reason makes Guddy feel nauseous. She has been waiting for Sara to finish her graduate degree, for the perpetual limbo of graduate student life to end. But Brooklyn is a great place to be in limbo and now it occurs to Guddy that she might not want it to end. Where will the market take them? Is Canada a possibility? Guddy has been trying to get back to Vancouver to be near Therese for a few years now, but Vancouver isn't Canada. Aiming for Vancouver in Canada is like tossing a dart in the dark and expecting a bull's eye.

And can she really go back, west coast or not? Can she, as Therese always says, take 'it,' meaning where she can't be at the moment, with her? What is 'it' about Brooklyn that she can't live without? What can she take? Do the firemen, who along with the sparrows, the local lunatics, her Cuban neighbour Daisy, coming in now with 'the girl,' her charge of some ten years whom she still neglects to call by her first name (does she have one?), cheer her on a daily basis? Does she need that?

And what should she leave? Diane, the Grey Gardens character who lives across the street? Sara helped her with groceries one day. Then a week or two after tried to help her sort out some kind of billing problem with Con Ed. After the woman bolted the door behind her she discovered that the house was in shambles, uninhabitable by any standards. There was no first floor, only the looming and, she was sure, rat-infested basement with a sumac growing in it. She took a deep breath when Diane pocketed the key and felt she could taste urine. But all she could do was follow her up to the third floor, the only inhabitable floor, at least in theory, for it too had a gash in the back, and there was, she realized, no bathroom, or apparently not one that worked. There was an oven but it had clothing stuffed in it. How do you cook, she asked before she could think better of it, and before she saw the hot plate, at which point Diane replied, Are you here to judge me or help me, because if it isn't the latter you need to leave.

And speak of the devil, she arrives, and is helped out of the car by a young driver with a wide, Mayan face, whom the old lady swats at before disappearing into the remnants of her home.

Sara puts a cup of tea on the desk, touching her shoulder as she passes. 'Take your running shoes,' she says. 'You should go for a run if you can, it will calm you.'

She carries a photograph of her sister. In it she is waving down from her balcony on Pendrell, just a few months ago, okay, more like half a year ago, her face puffed from the steroids, a last-option treatment for the pain with manageable side effects but terrible repercussions, and no going back. This sudden turn of events now shouldn't be a surprise to Guddy, but her sister has been making goals and reaching them these past seven years, so she had no reason but to believe she would make it to the fall and her big goal: her fiftieth birthday.

It's the goals that keep her going, a friend said, making them, realizing them. All winter the planning for summer, and so on. Optimism is for lightweights, Guddy thinks, it's goals that work. Tangible goals. But then, no, goals are a pragmatic kind of optimism. Like the endless upright avenues of Manhattan laid out long before they were needed. There is always a thin line between optimism and denial.

The previous summer Guddy had spent an entire month in Vancouver and much of it with her sister. They hiked up Cypress Bowl, walked through the forests on the North Shore, leaves crunching underfoot they were so dry, a fact that depressed both of them, though they tried not to dwell on it. In any case it was certainly not only the dryness or the heat that made them both uncomfortable, at least in the beginning. They sailed to Bowen Island, walked Spanish Banks, walked from Sunset Beach to Third Beach, walked the Drive, shopped at Granville Island, documenting, documenting, documenting. They spent time in Therese's garden, a tidy box in Mole Hill, a new co-operative housing project off Thurlow in the west end. Therese was happy, Guddy realized, finally, really, truly happy. There was an ease between them Guddy had not felt since she was a child with unwavering adoration for her older sister. The photo was the last moment of their time together. Guddy took it just before reluctantly driving off. She drove around Stanley Park until she could stop crying, and if she lets herself start now, she thinks, that will be the end of her.

Not now, her sister would have said if she had seen the tears. But if she did, she did not let on, and stood at the balcony waving and smiling as Guddy backed out. Later she sent an email saying simply, I was surprised at how sad I was when you drove away.

Why do we leave? And when is leaving abandoning?

She remembers the moment of leaving the west coast for good. She had not really thought of it as for good, more like a few semesters at grad school, but as the plane filled up and all around her buckles and accents snapped, she realized that she would likely never be able to come back. Not to the life she had. She would grow and change. It would no longer fit. She would want something else and though she wanted something else, she wanted it incrementally, selectively. This did not feel incremental. In a panic she unfastened her belt – but just as she was pulling her bag down, a flight attendant appeared at her elbow with a stern look.

She sat down, embarrassed. She was in a panic. But if she closed her eyes and breathed, she knew she had to go. She wanted to grow. She wanted to push herself, to disentangle herself from the narratives she'd become so entrenched in. She thought of a good friend's brother, a heroin-addicted fisherman (apparently not an uncommon thing, she was surprised to learn), and how he had to leave the industry, the city, every tie he had, in order to break his addiction.

Change is not a half-measure affair. Growth is not an afternoon sprint. One has to tunnel deep, or sever, and the past is allergic to these things, the past wants more of the same. So she took a deep breath and let herself be carried away by the momentum she had created. And she was right. She had not returned. Not for more than a visit. And those visits had largely been taken up by cancer: her father's, Therese's, then her father's death and trying to console and settle her mother who would not be consoled or settled. The other, more minor crises burned quietly in the background, but the visits were rarely about Jerry, or Bjarne, or Annie for that matter. What a family the Combals were. Everyone needed attention.

Particularly Bjarne, who was like a small elf you wanted to put in your pocket before he slipped between the cracks and disappeared for good.

Cancer is not for sissies either, she thinks. She is in a taxi heading toward La Guardia, with fresh figs and coffee from Sahadi's, tins of valentine hearts and chocolate kisses for her sister, having left Sara a diet-friendly present of red, heart-stitched, matching dishcloths that she realizes now is probably an affront even for her pragmatic partner. Her father had once bought her mother a toaster for Valentine's Day and she had never, ever let him live it down.

She takes in the skyline. Tomorrow the Empire State Building will likely be glowing cinnamon-heart red for Valentine's Day. Therese had wanted to visit New York on the first anniversary of 9/11 when they were practically giving tickets away. There were many logical reasons Guddy said no: the beginning of the semester, the heat, the persistence of the city, her health. Guddy kept imagining Therese on the subway overcome with nausea, or falling ill on a street in Manhattan and them having to navigate the hospital system.

Therese refused to speak to Guddy for months.

She had given in eventually, but she had never really forgiven Guddy: 'You have no patience, you've never been there for me. If you hadn't abandoned me that summer I wouldn't be on Prozac now, and if I hadn't gone on Prozac the tumour in my chest wouldn't have grown, and if the tumour hadn't grown it wouldn't have accelerated the spread of cancer and I might not have had to lose my breast ... '

That pre-Prozac year she had systematically cut herself off from all of her friends, and in a way that was good because it made way for Prozac, which made way for Helen, and with Helen, Therese thrived, and with Helen she went back to her friends, slowly, and with new dimensions, realizing that it didn't have to be all or nothing. She and Helen had several happy and productive years despite round three. The cancer she is dealing with now.

Once out of the taxi, Guddy moves quickly. La Guardia is easy. There is never a line at the Air Canada counter, where she stands, one step closer, though no, this portion of her ticket is actually United, so she has to drag her luggage to a slightly longer line.

She hands over her passport and e-ticket. Beside her a little girl peers out from under where she is crouching by her mother, and Guddy is back in Joe's room the morning he died, peering out from under his bed – ridiculous, she can hear Sara say, but the closer to family the clearer, more persistent the memories are.

They had never gotten over Joe. Not really. None of them. The house the morning after his death vibrated with some-thing she felt too sharply in her skin for too long. Everything – the air, the linoleum – all seemed held in suspension. She hid under the bed all that morning while her mother wailed, peering out at the high, spare ceilings of his room. She counted the length of the screams, the intervals. Then she closed her eyes and felt them rolling over her like waves. First the wailing was acidic, then like glass shattering, then it shook the house. She felt it coming at her until she ingested it and it became part of her breathing, regular in and out, waves of crying as she heard her father walking in and out of the room, then the doctor, and then the priest, trying to console her mother.

The hours passed, her siblings' feet came up the stairs, stopping momentarily at the closed door, then down again. The afternoon lengthened. Model planes flew above the bed in small circles. The sun moved across Joe's room, until the closet swallowed it.

Suddenly the crying stopped, and in a burst of joy she got up on her brother's bed and began to jump, because that is what they did, she and her brother, he at the side with his hands on her back, and she on the bed, jumping so high she could do somersaults. And then her father was there, grabbing her, shaking her over his head: *Your brother is dead. Don't you see that? He's dead. He isn't coming back anymore. Tomorrow he will be lowered into the ground in a box and gone forever, and now you have to be silent.* Then Annie, taking her by the hand into her and Therese's bedroom where they sat, on their beds, against opposite walls.

Were her sisters always there for her, she wonders, dragging her luggage through to security. Yes, she thinks, absolutely, yes. She hands her ticket and passport to a young woman, distracted, joking with two other officers. It's a rare moment of relaxation in a city exhausted from high alert, weary of guardedness and all of them understanding, at least on some level, the uselessness of the undertaking.

Guddy slips her boots off and puts them in a plastic tub. She takes out her laptop and places it on top of her coat and a security guard reaches out and takes the laptop, placing it in a tray of its own. And so, she thinks, childhood sneaks from one container to the next, one closet to the next.

She steps through the metal detector and is swiped with a stick – outlined, or benediction – and after the final nod she is off to reassemble herself. She is thinking about Judith Butler, whom she has heard give more than one lecture, and whom she had once run into in a bathroom, both of them searching for an acceptable glimpse in the mirror. That was in Princeton. She had been talking about terror post-9/11. She had been to Israel. She said something about the fallacy of neutrality, a concept Guddy wishes she could relate somehow to her sister Annie and her two daughters who argue that Guddy and Therese are political whereas they are neutral. It was well after the Bill Maher comments, well after the thaw had begun and people could have conversations once again. Butler was talking about mourning, and Guddy remembers thinking that mourning can become so many things – a way of being, of healing, or a weapon.

What happens with chronic mourning? She can still find herself small, standing in her brother's winter boots, pretending to be on a spaceship, or hiding in her childhood closet, fingering the fringes of her sister's tunic, imagining rare alien skins, because aliens surely have a variety of skins for all occasions: thick skins for childhood, thicker skins for courtship, flowery skins for travelling through galaxies. If men had been to the moon they must have found women there already, setting up house, decoding the atmosphere, wearing shifts and neon heels.

'Hold on,' a security guard says, dabbing her laptop and analyzing whatever it is the swab picks up from electronic devices. She floats back to Joe's room, his collection of model cars, his racetrack, set up under the bed and where she can, if she wishes, stick a foot out and make the cars tumble off and hit the wall at great speeds, which really, really pissed him off. Death magnifies odd moments. Makes things solid.

Why is what keeps her up at night. The wondering. Why a given event, why a given way of handling an event? *It's no good to ask why*, her Grade 11 algebra teacher kept telling her. *Don't ask why, just do as I say*, her mother said. *Why ask why*, had become her therapist's mantra. *Don't ask why, why ask why*, and yet it was *why* that fuelled her. Why did this happen? Why is she like that? *Why*, it seemed to Guddy, was the beginning of story, *why* is the conflict, *why* is the fuel.

If you tell my story, her mother says after a long story involving several farm cats, a cousin, lilacs and a burning haystack, *If you tell my story I will sue you. I swear to God, I will sue you.*

But my life is my story.

Your life is my story.

But I am here, apart from you, she is thinking, I exist apart from you.

I created you. One tug. She feels a snap at the waist and stops dead, right there in the terminal. *You see? One tug and you are back inside.*

She remembers hearing a man on the radio telling about an incident on a highway. He found a child clinging to the rear window of a car as it sped down the highway. He thought at first that he was seeing some kind of construction flag, then he thought perhaps a bit of something snagged on the rear wiper and, curious, he caught up to see what it was and saw a face. The car sped up. He sped up too, not quite believing what he was seeing, but yes, it was a little girl clinging, he could see, with at least one hand on the rear wiper blade. He sped up, the driver sped up and when finally he caught up the clinging child looked over at him from under her windswept hair, he said, and gave him the most intense look, a look he would never forget, he said, it wasn't a look of fear, or even of worry … but of … what? *Help me?*

Of course it wasn't *Help me*, Guddy thinks, dragging her luggage along. It was *Leave us alone.* It was *She is angry, yes, frightened, but she will come around.* And she might have come around, might have stopped on her own accord, though when the witness finally encouraged her to pull the car over he found another child in the back, a baby strapped into a car seat, and a wailing, wailing mother, about to kill herself, or the child, or all of them.

After a turbulent flight ending in a half-hour of circling the airport, their plane is the last to land. O'Hare is officially snowed in. She is sent to a hotel nearby. Thankful as she is to be warm and able to sleep if she wants, she is too wracked with guilt to relax. The Combals do not have layovers. They do not fly, nor do they sleep in crisis; they continue on, no matter if they have to crawl with torn limbs dragging behind ... Her mother would stop at nothing to see her father, or her own mother, when she felt the urge, or had some inkling of danger or illness: they'd take off in the middle of the night to drive across western Canada, or from one end of British Columbia to the other. She would scam a cab driver in Paris, she would steal her neighbour's pickup when her car was out of commission, she would hire thugs to move her furniture, she would do what it took.

Sure she might have caused the crisis, but no matter, Adel rose to the occasion. She would run through hell for love: the hotter, more daunting the trial, the better. And here Guddy is in a bed, in a hotel, when she really needs to be at Therese's side. Why isn't she out there clearing the runway? Why hadn't she taken a bus? She should have stayed at the airport, pacing.

She drifts off very briefly into a dream concerning a hospital of the uncared for. Old women lie abandoned in their beds, open-sored, crying into their pillows. At one point she has to walk over the beds themselves while the old women wail under her. This isn't a hospital, she realizes, and then a slam in the hallway wakes her. Some moment of anger, a dispute, the kind of thing that turns ugly in hotels, though perhaps not this one – an airport hotel in Chicago is not the same as the hotels and motels her mother could afford to run off to, the kind with bars on the main floor and strange, drunken men stumbling in and out. She can see only the parking lot from her window, a thin line, possibly the airfield, and the snow, which has been falling all night.

She may be guilty in general, but she has not done anything specific. She did not kill her brother. She did not abandon her mother, or her sister, for that matter. She has had these bad dreams, these dreams in which she barely escapes her childhood home by chance really, floating out of an upper window, before it bursts into flames. She tries to put the fire out. She tries to get back in the house. She tries to yell to her siblings but they can never hear her. Or when they do, they don't seem to see her: she has literally flown the coop. She is living her life, she tells herself, she is simply living her life. And that doesn't mean having turned her back. Not at all. In fact, she will be home in a matter of hours now, unless there is another snowstorm, but the sky is clear and she feels a sense of movement, of something having shifted.

She is thinking of Therese's anger. How she can become so rigid with it. Wield it. In the car, holding her book up to block out the view that is her mother and the highway weaving, complaining about the cigarette smoke, the way Adel would never let them open a car window because the draft gave her pneumonia. Therese sulking in the back because she has been taken from school and her Birdland friends perched on Oriole Crescent and Canary Drive, tucked along the Surrey side of the Fraser River with its log booms and sawmills; angry because she is in high school and dating, because she knows that families are meant to stay put, she knows that her mother's constant uprooting is not good, she knows that location is all, location is what will allow her to be a teenage girl concerned with boys and grades, which is what she wants even though she says she will not get married, why would she, her mother, their mother, has ruined the idea for her, forever and always, and finally, because Adel is the stupidest woman in the world.

Not that *they* have ruined it. Their father is never blamed, never included in the list of problems, it is the mother, her refusal to anchor, to tie her apron springs to a tree and hunker down, as if domesticity would proceed in an orderly fashion if she only gave in. Their father stands at the foot of progress, levelling the forests, smoothing the way for strip clubs and strip mines and strip malls. Astute, fundamentally pure in his belief in progress, their father is dedicated to its success, to its purest realization. And their mother? Dedicated to love. A rough, reckless, exuberant love, but love nonetheless.

'There are laws about parenting,' Therese yelled, pounding the window to get out.

And she was right, or ahead of her time: it's impossible to imagine five children in a car with a chain-smoking mother who refused them air.

She suspects that her sister would have killed her mother if she'd had the opportunity. 'What you need is a good fuck,' her mother had announced one night at dinner when Therese, at fifteen, was being particularly difficult.

If it bothered Therese she didn't let on: 'Isn't that what you need, Adel? Isn't that why we're always being dragged back and forth after your husband? So you can have sex?'

Her mother and her sister threw plates, lamps, knives at each other. Adel upended the table after a nasty comment from Therese about her gambling habit and their lack of clothing. 'You think I'm going to clean up your mess yet again?' Therese yelled.

And she didn't. She walked out, and after her came all of her belongings, emptied out of the closet and down onto the street.

Guddy worried Therese and Adel would both come to a violent end. They were variously in love or enraged with the world. They knocked back at it, were not averse to tripping people up, taking on situations well out of their depth, unwinnable fights, impossible arguments. They held nothing back. Their responses were visceral. Their aim, deadly.

Others look at her sister, her eyes, her dark hair and wide brow, and they see brightness, they see potential. But there in the back seat of childhood, she is steaming. She would never kill anyone, it is metaphor Guddy is indulging in, but she has seen and felt the rage boil to such a level. She has seen the knife blade stuck in the wall inches from her mother's head. Rage is a buffer for them both. Anger a fuel. Not the only fuel, but the fuel of choice, or at least of habit.

Once she and Sara woke to her sister's anger, coiled in the living room ready to wrap herself around them and squeeze the life out of them. She seemed to have literally blocked the sun. They stepped into the room, and stepped right back, cowering in the bedroom much of the morning. Then some hours later, when the light returned to her body, Therese called in to say she was making coffee and did they want any. It seemed impossible to trace that darkness. There she was, benign as a sunflower, wanting to go for lunch.

'I think about the stories you will tell after I am gone,' Therese had said then, just the two of them having coffee because Sara was too freaked out by the darkness and had left for the rest of Therese's visit.

'What makes you think I will tell stories?'

'You always find a way to spin things into gold. Why shouldn't something good come of all this?'

She has travelled from Brooklyn to Vancouver, door to door, in less than eight hours, but today, after sixteen hours in transit, she is still sitting on the tarmac in Seattle after yet another delay. She can't read, sleep or think; is determined not to let her mind drift back. Not to look out the window to the wing, where she imagines her father circling and circling, like a puppy looking for a good place to sleep. After Jean passed away, she often bumped into him, shoeless, carrying a brown paper bag, looking dazed. He never recognized her, never quite seemed to know where he was.

She dials her brother Jerry, regretting it the moment she hears his voice, and then feels awful about her reaction. She calls her sister Annie, which goes better. She tells her almost everything, but not all, since Annie will see Adel, and who knows what Adel might get out of Annie, and with that information, what she might do. 'I'll call when I arrive,' she says.

Just go, she thinks, willing the plane forward, and then tries to relax, to create some space between desire and the reality of her situation. Once she managed to achieve quite a bit of space between thought and action, now she sees that space has shrunk and again she is all reaction. Fuck Pema Chödrön, she thinks. Fuck Chögyam Trungpa Rinpoche. Fuck excessive patience.

When the plane descends over the Georgia Strait, she sees the rugged Sisters staring down over the muddy mix of the Fraser, the plane's shadow moving across log booms. Once on the ground, she begs her way through to the short customs line, and she is out to her friend Jake's old Datsun workhorse within minutes. 'Unbelievable timing,' Jake says, throwing her luggage in the back. 'Your room is ready.' She doesn't stop, as she usually does, to let the air sink in, but she feels it sweep across her face and it makes her dizzy and relieved that no matter how much Vancouver grows, that doesn't change. No, she doesn't want to stop for lunch, or even to drop her bags off and see Ruth, which is fine, Jake says, understandable, and within minutes they have scooted down Oak Street and she is walking into Vancouver General. 'Hospice is that way,' a security guard says, pointing down a hallway, a separate elevator.

And that is when it hits her: this was never about Therese going home. How could she have been so stupid? How could she have not seen that this was Therese's way of keeping her at bay? How had she not heard it in her voice? How could she have been so casual? Not come back over the holidays? Left Therese alone? Therese probably made Helen wait until it was too late for Guddy to arrive in time to say goodbye. Nothing personal. Perhaps she didn't want the bother of old wounds.

'Therese Combal,' she says, once out of the elevator, and a tall man steps forward from the bank of nurses. 'She's here,' touching Guddy's elbow, guiding her. 'Just over here.' And there is Helen, looking regal. But she has been crying. 'Don't tell me,' Guddy says. 'No, no,' Helen says, wiping her eyes, 'she's still here. You can see her.' And she follows Helen in, and there is Therese, asleep in a cool room with a view of the Sisters, smelling, as usual, of Pears soap and lavender. Her face, widened and puffy from the steroids, still exudes a sense of urgency, of curiosity in the mouth. There are flowers in several vases, crayon drawings on the wall. A set of clothes hung on the bathroom door, a heart-shaped box of chocolates open on a seat.

'They had to give her something,' Helen whispers. 'We'll talk when you want.' She closes the door behind her and there they are, together again. She and her sister. The silence, the cold room, the wide shiny green floor tiles, her sister, still but for the breathing, the odd twitch. She touches her cheek, cool, and moves to pull the blanket up before stopping herself. Her sister prefers things loose, cool; it is Guddy who is cold. And then another realization, Guddy feels as though she has been climbing for years, and now is about to descend, her body, accordingly, gearing down. She goes out to the hall, where Helen stands with a nurse.

'She isn't going to wake up, is she?' It comes out more forcefully than she intends.

Helen reaches for her hand.

'That's up to you,' the nurse says. 'I can let her wake up again, but she will be in pain.'

'We can talk about it,' Helen says. 'It's all too fast. You should take some time.'

'We gave her an injection,' the nurse says, 'just over an hour ago.'

'She was in tremendous pain. She was extremely agitated; she couldn't get comfortable.' Helen squeezes her wrist. 'She knew what she was doing.'

No, Guddy thinks, no. She wasn't sitting on the tarmac in Seattle when her sister checked out, for Chrissakes, why wasn't she here sooner? 'I don't understand,' she says, aware suddenly of something tearing beneath her.

'We can talk about it.'

'I was just talking to her two days ago,' Guddy says, more to herself than anyone else. 'She was talking about a hospice team at home.'

'Your sister has been very brave. I'm going to let you two talk and you can find me in the station if you have any questions.'

They are sitting in the hallway, Helen calm in a teal armchair. Guddy watches the light come through sheer curtains at the end of the hall, listening as Helen outlines in more detail the last week. 'Therese was lucky to get a bed,' she is saying. She had been going downhill for some time, but no one knew how badly until Helen dropped by with some soup.

'Why didn't she say anything?'

'I'm not sure she knew, or was lucid.'

'Was she coherent today? Did she know I was coming?'

'She did.'

Silence is so loud, Guddy thinks, releasing each of the endless thoughts that arise and need not be said.

'She wanted to see you,' Helen says. 'You were the only other person she said could visit.'

Not now, Guddy tells herself. 'You probably need a shower,' she says to Helen. 'You should go home, rest.'

'Are you okay here?'

'Yes. I'm fine here. I'm fine.'

'It's a matter of time now,' Helen says.

They both sit. Guddy painfully aware of the energy she must be giving off. Shut it down, she tells herself, contain. Focus.

'Would you let her wake up?'

'I understand that you want to say goodbye,' Helen says, gathering her things.

She sits by the bed, thinking, at first, that silence is best. For a long time she is still, watching her sister sleep, but now that she is still, the rush of thoughts slows, and in the space, huge sorrow begins to bloom, overwhelming her with surges of emotion. She braces against the tears, and each time she does, Therese twitches. It is never the right time to be emotional around Therese, she thinks, which makes her laugh, and then choke with guilt. She goes out of the room and comes back in when she has recovered.

She isn't sure what the right approach is. Stillness. Coming and going. But she also isn't sure she has a choice, or that there is a right approach. She moves between uncontrollable sobs and fits of hysterical laughing. There is nothing funny, but she keeps thinking of things Therese has said. 'What is she going on about,' she had said when a mutual friend was inconsolable. 'It's only her mother.'

Was she was always so flippant about death, or was it mothers?

Her cellphone vibrates and Guddy slips out into the hall.

'How and where are you?'

'I'm here, I'm fine. She's sleeping. I don't really know what to do.'

'You don't have to do anything,' Sara says. 'Just be there.'

'Yes, I'm doing that. But they gave her a shot before I came. You know, just before I came. And they are going to give her another one in a few minutes, and then every two hours until her system shuts down.'

'I'm sorry.'

'And so I won't be able to say goodbye. I mean I'm here, I want to, but they don't know if she can hear me.'

'I'm so sorry.'

There is another long pause and Guddy knows they are both righting themselves. They are so calm she feels a wave of guilt: she isn't suffering enough. She needs to be in more pain than she is.

'Guddy?'

'It isn't fair,' she says finally.

'No,' Sara agrees. 'It isn't.'

'How are you? Where are you?'

'I'm in Phoenix, it went well, so we'll see. Meanwhile, I know it's not the right time, but I got an offer.'

'You're kidding?'

'Isn't it incredible? So we have to talk.'

'I can't talk about this. I'm proud of you, but I can't – '

'I know. I mean, it went well today, but who knows, and Phoenix – '

'Yeah, not so into Phoenix.'

'But would Philadelphia be any better?'

'It's closer to New York,' Guddy says, trying to ward off the waves of guilt associated with having at least a theoretical future –

'It's not a great school.'

'It's not Arizona.'

– and a fussiness about that future.

36

'We just have to find out about health care. They want an answer pronto. I mean we can think about it, but – '

'Listen, I can't do this. Not now.'

'I know, I'm sorry, this is terrible timing. But we need to think about it. And soon. I'll be in my room all night if you want to call back.' Pause. Pace. 'Hello?'

'Should I let her wake up?'

'What do you mean?'

'I mean, should I ask them *not* to give her the next shot?'

'I don't know, Guddy, what did the doctor say?'

'There are no doctors, only nurses, and they say it's up to me.'

'Then it's up to you.'

'But she'll be in pain. She'll be in pain, but I want to say goodbye.'

'It's up to you,' Sara says.

'Happy Valentine's Day,' Guddy says, hanging up, and then stands with the phone in her hand for a long time before she can move. When she does, she slips back into the room. She tries sitting, tries standing. Takes a chocolate from the box and lets it rest on her knee. She closes her eyes. There is not a peaceful cell in her body. She eats the chocolate. Then another. She stands, staring out the window at her sister's city. 'We'll probably be in Philadelphia next,' she says finally. 'Can you imagine that? The City of Brotherly Love?' Why all this moving when she really would rather just stay here? But Vancouver isn't an easy place to stay in. Easy to come to, if you have money, but not an easy place to remain.

Her sister wanted to leave too, had tried to leave so many times – lived in Paris, Toronto – but she couldn't leave her city, not even for her career. She loved it too much. All its corners, which she touched so often, cycling, driving, kayaking; even when it didn't seem to support her as an artist, she loved it. She photographed it, framed it, moved through its shades and textures, as if it were part of her. And Guddy loved it too. So deeply she ached every time she left it. It was certainly the most beautiful city on the planet: she believed it could also be the smartest. They both did. And this constant dialogue about what could happen, what could be done, kept them animated always. 'It's such a beautiful view, Therese,' she says.

'It's good that you talk to her. She can probably hear.' The nurse has appeared. He stands behind her with a tray in hand.

'You think? I don't know if I'm saying the right thing. It all feels wrong.'

'I'm sure you are saying just the right thing. She can't respond physically, but the vital signs – '

Guddy is not sure she has seen any signs. Someone has trimmed Therese's bangs, she notes, and not evenly. The small scar left over from chicken pox in her right eyebrow seems larger somehow, her lips slightly chapped.

He holds the tray up. 'It's time for the shot.'

'Can we wait?'

'You want to let her wake up?'

'If she wakes up and she's in pain, if she's suffering, how long will it take to stabilize her again? I mean, if you give her a shot will she be out of pain instantly?' She can't believe she is asking this.

'Twenty minutes.'

'Twenty minutes?'

'She will be in pain for twenty minutes.'

She hears the *will*, not *might*, but tries to ignore that. 'Do you mind?' He affirms her choice with a nod and backs out of the room.

And so she waits, watching the Sisters fade and the lights on Grouse Mountain take the spotlight. She waits, trying not to think of the fact that she might never meet her sister's eyes again, or hear her voice, even that impatient noise she makes when Guddy is being sentimental or obvious.

'I'm thinking of your garden,' she says. 'The clematis on your back deck.'

After years on waiting lists for subsidized housing, Therese had finally found something she loves and can afford, and can live in, in Vancouver. It's small but elegant and fresh, and not out in Burnaby, or slotted in on some busy street corner. It's also in the west end. Small, but well designed. She has sunlight and two decks. She had finally been able to plant perennials.

Therese kicks at the sheet. What would she say if she were lucid? *Quit being indulgent?* She moves her chin sharply, exhales impatiently, snorts, rears. Guddy loosens the sheet at the bottom of the bed. She stands, holding her sister's hand, but again Therese strains, pulls away, flings her arm, jerks her leg, then kicks again, more violently. Guddy puts her hand on her forehead. Clammy. Then a sound, not at all pleasant, followed by a gurgle in her breathing. She checks the time on her phone. It's been only twenty minutes since the nurse left, but already Guddy is beginning to panic. Five more minutes, she tells herself, but the kicks become more violent. The phone rings and she sees it is Annie. She walks out into the hall.

'I've been waiting for your call,' her sister says.

'I'm sorry, it's rough, it took me by surprise.' Guddy sketches the details.

'Jesus,' Annie says, 'do you want me to come down?'

'No. She has signed an order in any case. No one is allowed in but Helen and me.'

'They can't stop me, can they? There's a seven o'clock flight.'

'Look, I've asked them not to give her the shot. If they give her another shot she won't wake up, they don't know how long she'll remain in that state, but she won't wake up again and I wanted to say goodbye.'

'Guddy, you shouldn't be alone with this. I should be there.'

'I'm not alone,' Guddy says. 'You're all here, in some way. I just thought you should know. Is Mom okay? Did you tell her?'

'She's okay. No, I didn't tell her, but I think she knows.'

'You didn't tell Bjarne, did you?'

'No, I wouldn't tell Bjarne.'

Guddy goes back to the room and stands by the bed. Of course Adel knows. Adel knows everything. Senses everything. Feels everything. Her screams from the night Joe died are still vibrating in Guddy's chest all these years later. They've never spoken about it. Not really. Not even to say *Let it go*, or *We need to move on*. A few years after Joe died, Adel woke Guddy and Jerry up in the middle of the night. The car was packed and they were off, driving through the canyon in the dark, all the next day, as far as Medicine Hat, where she slept for a few hours at the wheel before downing a coffee and hitting the road again, stopping only for gas. When they got to Winnipeg she drove straight to Joe's grave.

It was the first time Guddy had seen the grave. There had been floods that spring, and the earth around his headstone was uneven. Adel flung herself down on the wet ground, plucking chunks of grass from around the stone, trying to make it even on the earth. Guddy can't recall how long Adel lay there, or what she and Jerry did aside from look busy and try not to think of Joe in the earth and all the images that went along with that. She hadn't realized it at the time, but now she knows that it had been a recent addition, that headstone. That Joe had lain in an unmarked grave. Her parents had had no money for a headstone when he died.

Adel had refused the insurance money that came. Every year all the kids filled out their little insurance forms and took them back to school: loss of a hand, $1,000, loss of a leg, $1,500, loss of an eye, $2,000, loss of life, $10,000. My son is not a dollar value, Adel said, tearing the cheque up in the

40

adjuster's face. Adel then spent the next two years scrambling for enough money to feed them. Sending them out to deliver flyers at a penny a piece. Such ridiculous decisions. None of this was worth thinking about. She was not going to be guilty of tending to the past more than the present.

She puts the back of her hand on Therese's brow, moist, her breathing laboured, as if there is a catch in her lungs. She tries to cough it out, but she can't. Guddy lifts her, but Therese scowls, thrashes her head, unconscious but still irritated. Her wide face, eyes set apart, a strong jaw and ebony hair that always reminded Guddy of Björk – the powerful Björk, not the victim Björk from *Dancer in the Dark*, a movie she had walked out of it was so painful. Eyes closed, thrashing, Therese was not going to take those steps peacefully. Nor should she. She is not blind. She is not in a coma.

Though Guddy couldn't be certain about comas. She had once, in her life before Sara, slipped into a kind of coma. The doctors never did explain it, but for three days she could not make any part of her body respond. She could hear everything: her ex-partner panicking next to her, the doctors discussing, nurses poking at her, trying things, a spinal tap one day, another the next; Therese by her side throughout, advocating, pushing them to get a specialist; and then, on the third day she woke, craving a cheeseburger and ending her seven vegetarian years.

What was it? They had no idea. She had no epiphany when she woke. Not right away, in any case. She was so weak, so lethargic they put her on bed rest. She lay on a sofa with her pet rabbit on her chest. Finally someone told her she was watching her life slip away. I am? *Yes, you are a ghost in your own life.* After that she left Vancouver, left the west coast, left her life.

She thinks of Joe, in a coma for nearly two days before he passed, and her father, who also slipped into a coma for some hours before he passed. She had not been able to say good-bye to either of them. But there is part of her that believes Therese might still be hearing her. 'If you can hear me, squeeze my hand,' she says every now and then. But nothing.

A rush of emotion wells up in her at the thought of her sister's dogged loyalty. Not now, she tells herself, not now. Suddenly she remembers her sister paddling up behind her one summer at a small lake they went to in northern Ontario. It was the first time Guddy and Sara had rented a cottage, and they flew Therese out to be with them – eight years ago now, but they thought then that it might be the last opportunity. It was August, warm, the water like a thousand silk sheets, one on top of the other. Every morning before breakfast Therese dove in naked; it was the first time Guddy had seen the scar where her breast had been, like a lightning bolt, vertical and angry.

One morning Guddy decided to swim across the lake alone. She always panicked for a moment right in the middle, when the water was deepest, darkest, and the wind came up strong. She had the sense that someone was watching her. She turned to see Therese in the canoe, paddling quietly behind her. She smiled, and Guddy felt herself overcome with grief, so much so that she suddenly could not swim. What would she do without her sister? She began to sink, to take in water, her body getting heavy, useless. So this was how people drowned. Therese paddled closer, and very calmly said, *Not now*. Guddy sputtered, choked, wanted to say something, but Therese simply repeated, *Not now*.

Guddy likes to remember that she followed that up with *I know you love me, Guddy, and I love you*, but that is not what happened. She sucked up the tears and swam.

She has made a mistake, she tells the nurse. She doesn't need to say goodbye. She doesn't need anything more from her sister. She follows the nurse and an orderly back into the room.

'She has water in her lungs,' he says. 'That is normal under the circumstances.'

'I'm sorry,' Guddy says. 'She's already more uncomfortable than she needs to be, I want you to give her the shot.'

'Are you sure?'

'I'm sure, please. It was the wrong decision.'

'It was a decision,' he says. 'You should leave now. I'll call you when she is stable again.'

She has been an absolute failure as a sister, she thinks. Even down to the end. Why couldn't she have let her go peacefully? Now they have to stabilize her. Her sister does not want other people making decisions for her. She wants a dignified end. Went to great lengths to ensure one. Signed the DNR. Wants no life supports. What was Guddy thinking?

She goes out to the small lounge for caregivers and relatives to find Susan, a good friend who has been a constant with Therese, talking to Jake. Jake has a coffee in each hand and when she sees Guddy, extends one, and then, thinking better of it, hands the coffees to Susan and grabs Guddy, squeezing her tightly.

I don't deserve this, Guddy thinks, wanting someone to slug her more than hug her.

'I didn't know,' Susan says. 'No one told me. I went to her apartment and no one answered. I used my key and no one was there. Helen never picked up. Then I found Jake at the dog park.'

'I'm sorry,' Guddy manages, not quite sure what to do with her body, or her words, or her eyes. 'It's all been so sudden.'

'Can I see her?'

'She's asked that no one be allowed in. You know how proud she is. She doesn't want people seeing her like this.'

'I need to say goodbye,' Susan says, but Guddy has slammed her mind into neutral and the words bleed together, making not sense, but music: of course she should see her, but it isn't up to Guddy. She nods along, trying to keep her face neutral.

The nurse appears again. 'You should come now.' Jake squeezes her hand quickly, and lets go.

The nurses have eased her, tightened the sheet up around her chest, laid her arms outside the sheet, at her side, but Guddy can hear that her breathing is still laboured. She leans over and pulls her as close as she can. She wants to tell her she can go, she has fought so hard and now she can let go, but all she can say is 'I love you,' and 'I'm proud of you.'

'I am so proud of you, Therese.' And she is. She is more proud than she ever knew. And as she squeezes her sister, she feels her take a deep, deep breath. A breath that seems to take every ounce of energy she has left in her body, but it dislodges whatever was blocking her lungs. And then she exhales.

There he is, he and his childhood sitting very still on the stairs. Heart thumping so hard he is surprised his sisters haven't heard. They hear things. They respond. They scurry in the night. He is wearing the pyjamas his aunt had bought for him and his brothers. Now brother. Now just one. His head is shaved. He runs his fingers along the nape of his neck, tightens himself into a ball. He is terrified of the gaping hole that has opened up in his childhood. Terrified, but compelled: he moves toward it like a tongue to a missing tooth, scraping, chafing.

He used to sneak down to his mother's bedroom at night for peanut brittle. Now he feels a pang of guilt for thinking of sweetness after Joe. There is something terrifying happening that he doesn't understand. He would like to erase it. He would like to not have feelings. He would like childhood to be more neutral, more clear in its procedures. More predictable.

He rode to Joe's funeral with his older cousins and they told him that all the blood is drained from a body when a person dies. The body is filled with chemicals so that it doesn't decompose. That is how they see his brother in his coffin, a husk that has been filled so it will not decompose. He understands about decomposition. He understands death.

There are sections in cemeteries set aside for children. This is not a part of childhood anyone wants discussed.

Someone has come and put thick metal bars over their house. Someone has come and turned the key on his childhood so that the earlier part is bulgy and about to burst and the new part is flat and without energy. The new part lags. It might be cut off.

He has not been able to shake the feeling that his life is over. He imagines childhood like a giant hourglass —

all of the molecules must pass through the small neck so he can come out the other side a man. He is missing some molecules. He has reached the mid-point too soon. Something is lodged firmly in the middle.

He cannot turn away. He listens until all he can hear is his mother, weeping. That is his childhood now. But it is not only him. No one, not even his father, seems to be able to imagine a future.

But he is not Joe. Guddy is not Joe. They are alive, here, in skin. Does this make them unique? Is Bjarne unique? Can childhood be unique? Individual? What is the equation of his brother's death and how can he understand it?

The questions hang in the air around him.

Later, the questions repeat in the odometer, unspoken.

Later, the questions repeat in cigarettes lit, extinguished, pieces of puzzle placed, pieces of plastic coming together in his model airplanes, bigger, more complicated, so huge they can fly through the air.

Or not. No, he suspects not.

Now they are heading west for a second chance. There was talk of this earlier, over dinner. Over many dinners. There was laughing even, when his mother told them they would live in a nudist colony in a forest, near the ocean, all of them, walking around without clothes, and Joe said for some reason he saw them all out there but not him. It bothered his mother, who stood up to knock on the wooden door frame, and in doing so, knocked the table and spilled milk everywhere and, flustered, served more peas when they already had too many peas rolling around, refusing to be forked.

His siblings purr in their rooms around him. His mother cracks sunflower seeds, a pyramid of shells in the ashtray helps to keep some parts of her brain smoothed. Of course she does not do that now, no, now she lies in bed, crying, trying to turn herself inside out. Now, from where he is perched, seventh stair from the top, knees so tight that if he tried to move he would tumble down the stairs loud and clumsy as a turtle, there is the screaming.

He is too old to be afraid. He would like to be in her arms, in her bed, but he is not allowed anymore. He is too big, and this pleasure is reserved for his baby sister, Guddy, who is probably in there now.

The disappointment is palpable. If you were on the stairs in such a moment you would know how it feels to hear the sounds of your inconsolable mother. You would understand the way one is suddenly kicked out of one's own childhood and sits watching it.

There it hovers, childhood, at the bottom of the stairway, a grotesque reflection of the many unspoken anxieties of childhood, the in-betweenness of event, the sudden flashes of unnamed feeling, the confusion of body, the difficulty discerning where one thing begins and another ends.

There is bravado and bluster but nothing about the night that is Take that, *or* Take this. *He would like to be much tougher than he is. He would like to unfurl, but he is so tight. Why these long nights? Why this silence that grows up around his bed? In the night*

48

there is only one destination, that pool of light that is
his mother's room, the cracking of the sunflower seeds,
the curl of smoke.

JERRY

S o what, Jerry is thinking. When is the last time anyone worried about him? When is the last time one of his sisters picked up the phone to see how he is? He has listened to all the details and says only that he can't be expected to drop everything because she, his sister, is coming to Vancouver, even if … what? What is really going on? She isn't being clear with him and he knows it. Not that it would necessarily change anything. He has been spurned. He has been spurned since the beginning, if there can be said to be a beginning, and that is what matters. He is sorry, yes, but what can he do now? This is how he feels. Pissed off. He doesn't say these things, he simply says *no*, and lets his sister simmer. Lets her marinate. And no, he thinks, it hasn't always been like this. He has arrived here and there is nothing he wants to say or think about it further. In fact, he would like to amputate the feeling. And family, for that matter, he would like to amputate feelings and family entirely. She says something about keeping him posted. Posted about what, she won't say. A hint of rage, of impatience, flares up briefly in each of them, and then she says she has to go, and so she does.

He lets the phone cradle his leg. Big fucking deal, he thinks. He is not happy at this very minute and doesn't need his sisters witnessing it. Things were going fine until recently. Now he finds himself in a slump, a minor slump perhaps, but it is wearing away at him. Living in a basement suite at his age? Well, it isn't what he expected for himself. He thought by now he would own his own house, be renting out his own basement to some poor fuck down on his luck. But no, he is the poor fuck. And now with housing prices skyrocketing and pre-Olympic real estate speculation going on to the degree it is, unless something changes and changes quickly, he will remain where he is, looking up from below ground, here with his new lady friend, an improvement over the last painful relationship he had wormed his way out of. How he had developed such poor taste in women is not a mystery, he likes to say, given he has two queer sisters and a hysterical, certifiable mother.

He snaps the phone onto its base. The truth is, he hasn't seen his sisters since his father's funeral five years ago, or soon to be five years ago, and naturally that was not pleasant. There was a service in Aldergrove. He went out in a cardboard box. Afterward, dinner at the White Spot. It was the first time they were all together like that since he can't remember when, and he and Annie downed two beers while they were haggling over the menu. Okay, not haggling maybe, not haggling, but otherwise engaged and so not likely to notice or comment on his every move, which they both liked to do. Therese had burst into tears in the middle of dinner, saying she would never forgive any of them for not letting her know their father was so sick, and Guddy, in particular Guddy, who had been the one to give the eulogy, such as it was.

They aren't a family that has much to celebrate. He had not indulged in a ceremony either time he married, and Annie stopped insisting they all show up after the second and hadn't bothered to tell him about the fourth. Now Guddy-two-shoes is on her way back to town. She said something about Therese, but he didn't want Therese in his life. She has been ill, yes, for that he is sorry, but she's a judgmental, nattering old hen, always critiquing his – and everyone's – life, and she has been sick on and off for nearly twenty years so that isn't new. She's always offering advice he doesn't want, has never asked for, when it's plain she can't navigate her own life.

If you can't accept me for who I am, you can fuck off.

Exactly what he said to his son before he moved out. That was two years ago and now look at him. Swaggering around with his Aston Martin. Wouldn't know how to slide through the window without Jerry. Wouldn't have an inkling, or care about horsepower, or paint colour (like, choose the pewter grey or the storm red, not white.).

52

He has not been the best father, the most attentive, but he has been consistent, he has remained relatively stable (aside from not providing either a mother figure or a regular income), and unlike Adel he has not dragged his son across three provinces, through snowstorms, fighting in restaurants and motels, on the side of the road, running to or from in the middle of the night. Nor has he made his son drive a Chrysler. No, his son had a childhood, imperfect though it may have been, and a little rough around the edges as he got older (frustrating little prick), but he had been given an education where cars were concerned.

He takes his keys down from the peg on the wall by the door and thinks about slipping out without Darlene, but then no, he presses himself against the wall and yells in at her. There is a scuffling somewhere in the bowels of the suite (a basement in a basement, imagine that).

'What?'

He raises his eyebrows, irritated by the way she says *what* instead of *yes*, which makes his neck twitch. At that she moves toward him, both hands on his shoulders, digging in. 'Ah,' he says so softly he can barely hear it, but she does. She hovers temporarily then digs in deeper. His whole spine and both shoulder blades are a constant source of pain and she does know how to ease it.

'You better have done those dishes properly,' he says, as if he is talking to a kitten. 'I'll check when I get home.'

She swats at him. 'Where you going?'

'Oh,' he says, 'you want to come with me?'

She hesitates.

'Come on,' he says. 'Grab your coat.' But before she can, he sees the Aston Martin pulling up out back. 'Well, will you look at that?'

Jerry's son, Nathan, outgrew him around the same age Jerry himself outgrew everyone in his childhood, only his son overtook Jerry by a good three inches, which meant he was hitting six-foot-six and of course was recruited for the basketball team. This gave Nathan a kind of social cachet that Jerry had never known. Jerry was supportive: drove him to the practices, sat through the games, took in the statistics, listened as his son told the coach, the girls, his teammates about his plan to design a line of less geeky, lace-less and flexible running shoes. He watched his son willow across the court and even worked out a training routine for him. A routine that included inviting his son to use his own personal training equipment – the upright bicycle (his only option for watching television), his personal weights, which he increased in number three times over the year of their training, adding another bench and specially moulded weights of his own devising. When his son did sit-ups, he did them with weights that lay like heavy lead armour on his chest.

Jerry counted as his son did push-ups, sit-ups and chin-ups. He boxed with him to increase his reach and agility. This wasn't conventional basketball training – it was cutting-edge, Jerry thought, and initially it seemed his son did also.

Nathan gets out of the car and stands beside it.

'Will you talk to him?' Darlene had no children of her own and the idea of parenting in any way was terrifying to her.

'Wait here.' Jerry slips out the sliding glass doors onto the wet concrete, which is slick with moss from the broken downspout his landlord isn't about to fix. He walks in his socks up the stairs (stupid) and stops at the gate, nodding at his son, who nods back as if he is catching something in the air. 'Well?' he says.

'Well?'

He has never been in the Aston. Not because he hasn't been invited, but because he has refused. 'How's the car?'

'Great.'

'No crashes?'

'Ha. You want to?' Again the nod.

Jerry cocks his head.

'So, how are things? Work? Darla?'

'Darlene,' Jerry snaps.

'Yeah. Saw her at the Shark the other night.'

'She wasn't at the Shark.'

'No, I was at the Shark, I saw her.'

'You mean in the Shark?'

'No, going in. I was going in and I saw her. Look, that doesn't matter. The truth is – '

'The truth?'

'The truth is, I've come – '

'You've come?'

'I need a favour.'

'Do you?'

'Yes, I need a favour. I need some cash.'

'You need some cash?' Jerry laughs.

'It's just – '

He still plays ball, Jerry knows, but at a public court, not, as they had dreamed, on a university team or maybe even the NBA. If he had made the cut, it might have been Simon Fraser, and he would have gone to the States, been playing all those fancy-ass colleges and what would Guddy have said then? Maybe his son might have passed her by on his ascent. Maybe he would be designing shoes now. Who knows?

'It's just – '

'Yes?'

'You know the people who got me set up? Well, they want their investment back and it's kind of sudden, you know, and I'm just not liquid at the moment.'

'You're not liquid? Where do you get this from?'

'Get what from?'

'This language, this attitude?'

'Look, I need cash is what I'm saying, Dad. I need some cash for a few weeks and I promise I'll pay it back with interest and if I don't – well, I'm willing to sign over the Aston.'

'You mean they want money?' And just as he says that he notices the deep purple creeping around his son's right eye. 'Jesus, Nathan. What the fuck?'

'It's not a big deal. Look, I have two units on the market. They could go tomorrow. It's just not a great location this time, a stupid location and – who knew, you know? It worked before, now we have these units sitting. It's like a little dead patch. Everything around is selling. And Aces says it's because the buy-in is too high so now everyone is looking at markets as far away as Saskatchewan – '

'Everyone? Aces? You work with a guy named Aces?'

'Do you have any idea how many units sold in the last month? Everywhere you look, imagine that, multiplied by ten in terms of people. It's endless.'

'Well, if it's endless, what's wrong with your units?'

'No Starbucks. People think they're on the moon.'

He is on the freeway, the tail end of it, or beginning, depending on which way you're going. Used to feel like the end of the world. That was part of why he liked the valley as opposed to the city. The city? Well, the city was greed; the city, as his father used to say, is where the greedy feed off the dumb. The rich get rich off the backs of the workers in more than one way: they have their bodies nine to five, but then they get a cut out of the food they eat, and they own the rooms they sleep in. Workers are the crumbs of the rich. His father never made a penny that wasn't directly linked to his labour; even when he had an innovation, he put it to direct use. He didn't want to be a landlord: he didn't believe in profiting off people's basic need to live.

And maybe more than anything, that is what has changed in the valley. Even more than the physical changes – and since they arrived in 1969, much has changed physically – it's real estate that has changed. They endured the Expo real estate frenzy, the Hong Kong frenzy, and now they have the Olympics. This on top of the selling of whole swaths of land, the dot-com market, the 'super natural' discovery of a 'world-classss' city, whatever that means. All that means, he recalls his father saying, is there won't be anything left for you or me. When the rich get excited, be worried. Be very, very worried.

People have prospered and he has not been one of them. Nor has his brother, nor have most of his relatives – the people he has known his whole life. The people who prosper in these situations are rarely working people like himself. Or they are people like himself who have won the social lottery: his cousin Stu who has a Mercedes dealership in Whalley, and Norman, who owns some kind of software company. They are people who have successful parents to bankroll them, or they are people from away who make a living off investments else-where. His son thinks he is one of them. Twenty-one and he makes more money in a month than Jerry can make in a year, but how can he keep that up? Where does money without any grounding get anyone? It's like being on crack.

What is his son proud of at the end of the day? How can personal wealth, with nothing to show for his labour but abs and deep pockets, be satisfying? Well, it isn't even labour, is it? He drives around, buying condos and selling them before they're even ready to occupy. Get rid of the middleman, is what Adel always says, and he himself has clearly taken that to heart, always trying to find a deal, trying to get ahead, but his son – he's operating at a whole other level. His son *is the middleman*, creator of nothing. His son is the slick talker who can put himself between you and your money more ways than you can say *overspend*. Jerry was confused at first. 'It's like those people who buy bulk hockey tickets and sell them for twice the price come game time,' Nathan explained. 'Only it's condos.'

'You mean those fucks everyone hates because they spike ticket prices? Those fucks? You're, like, scalping condos?'

'It's not just me, everyone is.'

'Oh, everyone is. How the hell did you ever get started? How the hell did you get two pennies to rub together?' He'd done someone a favour and they brought him into the game, that's what he said. He had hidden money, in other words, let them use his name. Open an account. Hide transactions. The valley has no shortage of pricks like that, taking advantage, only most of them are in office, most of them are on the five o'clock news talking about preserving lands in the GVRD, and then meeting developers for drinks in Yaletown. He wants his son to do well, but not this way.

Jerry might have made different choices if he had come from a different place, but yeah, yeah, yeah, he thinks, whine, whine, whine. That's his sisters' hobby. Always blaming their lot on the shortcomings of their childhood. Not that there isn't some truth in it, and not that he couldn't go on and on about Adel and how she clipped his father's wings – clipped all of their wings – but if anyone should complain about their childhood it's him. He is the one who got the short end of the stick. But did he complain? No. He didn't want 'up' and 'out' of his situation. He wanted to do better, yes, but he liked being a worker. He wanted to make things, or at least provide materials for building actual things. His father got dirty. He went out into the world and had a look under the skins of our roads. He could calculate how much rock he'd need to crush, how many hours and men and gallons of diesel it would take to create that – he was out in it. At the head of progress. And as such, his father got more respect than his little prick son will get as long as he lives. Yes, his father was broken, had suffered in every part of his body; by the time he died he had shrunk eight inches, and it all went into labour. And what did that labour do? Fed him and Bjarne, and the trilogy of witch sisters. Oh, and yes, Adel. Certainly it fed and clothed and kept Adel in gambling money.

Does he think his father was perfect? No. Not always. Okay, not often. And maybe it wasn't a better time to live, but it had its moments. The vast tracts of land they found themselves in, finding a natural hot spring, he and Bjarne hopping boxcars. The summer travelling was good – even if it was always in a panic and even if it always involved cheap motels, mice, many of them, even in the beds at night, poking around his ears, and sleeping, all of them, in the same room often enough. Listening to Adel cry. Swimming in the ditches before they knew what a ditch was. Halloween mischief, firecrackers, piles of burning shit left on unfortunate doorsteps. Listening to Adel cry. His whole head burns when her name comes up. He long ago stopped thinking of her as 'mother,' though he thinks now, not soon enough. Should have left one of those burning bags of shit on her doorstep. He has given some of his best years over to her. He grips the steering wheel of his Jimmy. Somewhere, of course, Adel is crying. And somewhere his little prick son is taking a corner way, way too fast.

Next to him Darlene pushes closer, her thigh against his. Unlike his first few choices in women, Darlene has a way of feeling his pissed-off thoughts and soothing him. He appreciates this about her even if he is sometimes tempted to strike out at her in response. It isn't her. Not really. He is learning that he has an open nerve running through him; he has noticed that there is often no obvious connection between what someone is doing around him and the irritation he feels. In his defence, a doctor once told him chronic back pain can give you a short fuse, but now that he has recognized this pattern it irritates him even more. Particularly as he can't seem to change it.

Dead zone. His son had bought a condo in a dead zone. Even in this market it was still location, location, location. Hard to pick a bad location in the Lower Mainland, but apparently his son had found it. In a way, this early failure might be good. It might cure him of his lust for easy money.

He pulls in to Dunkin' Donuts, his favourite since he can drive through, and driving through means less in and out of the truck, and the less he moves his back the better. He gets a large coffee and an old-fashioned glazed. Nothing fancy. Another of his father's traits he tries to emulate. He settles in and decides that he will drive out to the end of the valley, all the way to Hope, where maybe he will take Darlene for lunch since, thanks to the roadside rose vendor, he remembers it's Valentine's Day, though he doesn't have to worry because he has a heart-shaped box of chocolates hidden at home. He has a big, 3-D card too. He likes buying cards. The bigger the better. He reads the lines in the drugstore and really thinks about the appropriateness. The match. It means something. His sisters, of course, do not appreciate this. They buy blank cards and write personal messages, but those messages seem to Jerry no more insightful than the words he's carefully chosen in the store.

He lied to his sister, telling her that he is going to work today. He is not. He is in between jobs, in between several things at once. Something about hearing her voice makes him want to dodge her. Besides, she came last summer and did she call him then? She had a dinner party at the house she was staying at in Kitsilano, and his son was invited, and Therese, and a cousin, and not him. You've always been grumpy, she had said on the phone, but now you sound bitter. This bothered him more than most of the things that came out of his little sister, and over the years plenty has bothered him: despite the distance, it had never occurred to him that she judged him.

He noses his Jimmy back out to the freeway. Darlene holds his doughnut for him and all he has to do is shift and she brings it up for a bite.

One thing he isn't is a hypocrite. Where his sisters are concerned there is plenty of that. Calling his son and not him, for one, but other things too. All squeaky on the surface, but then she goes behind his back and he knows she does. Why waste your time with Jerry, Guddy had apparently said to their father once.

If that's what they think of him, why bother? Why bother at all? It's true he has taken his share of help from his parents over the years, but he has also tried hard to be a dutiful son, a thoughtful brother. How do they think he feels when he visits his sisters and sees not one of the yearly family portraits he has sent them up on the wall, or on a bookshelf? Okay, no, he has actually not visited any of them in over a decade, but still.

All those attempts to connect with his father and what had he got? His father so desperate for peace of mind that the first sight of another human being to distract his wife and he was off to smoke a cigar in his little work shed, or off in his filthy van, burning down the highway to Mitchell Island where he occasionally worked.

How had his father managed all those years? Everywhere he went Adel was there behind him, her bad energy shitting all over, speaking out, making fun of him, embarrassing him, keeping him up all night with her dramas. Getting in the way of his father, of his relationship with his father, and ultimately, ultimately, giving his tools and his notebooks to someone else, not even family. She seemed bent on crippling his father and bent on keeping him down. Was it any wonder he broke when the old man died? Could he be blamed for calling her up and saying, 'You! You were the one who should have died.'

No. He doesn't suppose he should have said that, no. And no, he doesn't mean it, and yet he is completely unable to take it back. Even now. He may not ever see family again and who would notice? Not his sisters. And fuck you, Guddy, yes, I permed my hair in the nineties because it was oily and whatever the chemical process involved in perming is dried up my hair, and you know what? Plenty of women said that with my hair and moustache I looked like Tom Selleck, so eat shit.

Or something like that.

Now Nathan is bleaching his hair and plucking his eyebrows.

Jerry's father used hand soap on his hair. Never used a grooming product in his life. Walk like a man, stink like a man. His father was perfect that way. Himself? There always seemed to be something wrong with him. Wrong hair, wrong shoes, pants too short, wrong wife, wrong job, wrong attitude. Fuck. Had he ever, even in the beginning, been given a break?

No. Because there was never any beginning, only the relentless, silent rejection. That silence. That nothing. That lack of thought. He penetrated none of their lives. He was invisible. Her hand moving over his for another head. Always another head, older, younger. I was a gap, he thinks, I was a goose egg, I was forgotten, and I still am. I had no childhood. I had no moment of relief. I had no arms, I was nothing, a stick, something at the side of the path, not noticed.

Darlene nudges his elbow.

'There was a time … There was a moment, when we were happy,' he says.

She nudges again. 'When who was happy?'

But he does not answer. He is thinking of a brief moment when they had rifles and shot things in the woods. Bjarne was big, he had been working out. Bjarne was nimble, lower to the ground and elastic, but Jerry had the height on him. Bjarne could hit more forcefully but he could reach farther, and while he had the height, Bjarne could kick higher, there was no beating him in that, only avoiding. It was a great summer, a fabulous fall: overnight he was the tallest, even taller than his father, so tall his mother had to stand on her tiptoes to smack him.

All that summer, bottles lined up and shot, oranges tossed in the air and shot. He wanted a spring-piston gun, something that could shoot off rounds, but they had the single stroke, one step up from the Red Ryder BB Gun. Not enough. He wanted the feeling of the bullet piercing skin. It didn't have to be human. It could have been a bird, or a squirrel, or a cat. They argued about it all summer and never did it. Not intentionally anyway. Once Bjarne shot a cat by mistake and he broke down and cried. He couldn't handle the cat lying there, the pathetic tongue, *laa, laa, laaa.* Jerry was the one to put it out of its misery with another shot to the head. He was the one to bury it, not Bjarne.

Later, when they were in the Kootenays, he bought himself a .22 and he practised by himself until he could handle it, and then he and Guddy shot cans out back. Okay, he really didn't want to pierce skin. He really didn't. But at the time, he thought he did. He never did shoot animals. Not like Annie's first husband who shot deer from his window. Middle of breakfast and a deer shows in the yard? *Ka-ching.* A freezer full of meat.

Minutes later, seconds really, and they are in Chilliwack. They are moving too fast, or time has shrunk, distances have shrunk. Used to be a major day trip into the city from Chilliwack, now it's a suburb, now people commute in and out to work. No wonder there is always traffic backed up. He hasn't been here in months, years really, and what he sees he can't believe. Why should he be surprised after seeing what's happening in Surrey, Coquitlam, subdivision after subdivision, tucking them in tight as mice in a nest?

He pulls off the freeway and onto the old highway, past the rows and rows of hops. It's the slow route, and lined with fruit stands in the summer and fall. He doesn't drive it very often and when he does he is reminded of that first summer, the summer they moved to B.C., the summer after Joe passed away. They lived in a motel somewhere near here. Right by the lake, though of course they never went to the lake. That was their childhood, right by things but unable to take advantage, as if they were all tied around their necks to the mother, to the mother and her desire. For what? Preoccupation? Busyness? Numbing? Whatever it was it wasn't about them. After all, they all lost Joe, not only Adel. They all had their insides torn out. But no. Grief was Adel's province. Fuck. You. He thinks. Fuck. You. Her face right in front of him in the road.

Three times she dragged them back and forth from Vancouver to Winnipeg with their measly belongings in a trailer. They spent some time in the shadow of Little Mountain and that summer a prisoner broke out of the penitentiary and they were all on high alert. Now that he lives nearby he knows this isn't uncommon, but it seemed then as big a news story as the fact that men had landed on the moon. He was out there somewhere, lurking. He had killed a man with his bare hands. He had beaten a prison guard. Guddy in particular was terrified, convinced she could see him everywhere, hiding in the brambles, surviving on blackberries, and they all played it up, even Adel, showing up with a flashlight under her chin outside the bedroom window and tapping on the glass. He had shit himself.

In a manner, they too had survived on berries that summer. They had been picking raspberries, six of them in a small shack while their father was off looking for work. They were the only family on the farm, the other pickers being young Québécois who arrived in a caravan of vw vans and sat around long into the night singing. Therese refused to work the first day, saying it was illegal to make children have adult jobs. They should be exploring, as far as she was concerned, daydreaming, drawing, painting. Therese had won a colouring contest and was bent on being an artist. He and Annie wanted to work. They weren't afraid of the garter snakes in the fields. Bjarne wanted to work too, but not with them, already he had his eye on the second-in-command position.

Of course he wasn't there, their father. He was always working and yet barely able to put food on the table. That is the part that confuses and angers him. Clearly it was a choice *not* to be there, and the choice to be away wasn't worth it. Was it?

The hops go on in clean lines, bare now. When they first drove to the lower mainland they believed they were in paradise, even when they had nothing, and there is still something to that thought. The air is so sweet. The mountains make you feel protected and even when it's cold it isn't Manitoba cold – frostbite warnings, days when unless you have a block heater there's no way the car will start. And he still feels this way: standing in the valley, anywhere in the valley, and breathing in the air, looking up at Garibaldi. It's unbelievable. No matter how many people come, how many houses are built, how clogged up the roads become, not even if he has to spend the rest of his days living in a basement suite, he will not leave. This is the most golden place on earth and he is in it. He has his part. His small stake. It's about priorities. What a man values. Like Therese, he values where he lives, and he won't go anywhere else.

The old Yale Road goes past Hope. In the old days, everyone stopped at Hope. It's the gateway to the canyon, to the gold rush. It's not a hopeful place, though perhaps it once was. If you made it that far south, which meant through the canyon, you deserved to have hope: if you were heading north by foot, or mule, and about to hit the canyon, you might have needed hope. The rest of the canyon towns had great names: Alexandra Suspension Bridge, Hell's Gate, Boston Bar, Scuzzy Creek, where the first passenger train arrived in 1886, Fort Langley, the old Hudson's Bay trading post, the rush to gold in Barkerville, the old Yale road, the Cariboo road ... He still remembered the details because on road trips Guddy would quiz him from the details on her postcards.

They both loved the canyon. It was the Coquihalla of the day. Guddy kept postcards from every place they stopped. He sent her a few postcards over the years. Still thought about her when he passed a rack, and sometimes still bought one out of habit, though he had long ago stopped mailing them.

He thinks of her now, off in New York City, where from time to time he considers visiting her. But which Guddy would he find? The Guddy he knew is long gone. This person, this contemporary Guddy, whoever she is, has knocked his sister out cold and slithered into her body. He isn't comfortable around her. She lives with a woman he has never met and cannot understand, even the idea of her. Even now, when half of the characters on TV are so inclined, he does not understand the gay thing. Darlene thinks it's modern. Thinks his sisters are interesting. Novel, she said. It's novel to have a queer sister. Or two, as it turns out. He does not find it interesting.

But he is thinking now of the canyon. The curves. The sheer canyon walls. Some so crumbly they have to be covered in thick chain-link. He feels the urge to revisit them, take the corners just a little too fast and feel Darlene tense up and shift over to him, as if hanging on is either going to slow him down or save her if they crash. Not that he will crash. He has, after all, learned to drive from two speed junkies. Who liked speed more? Who could take a corner faster? Hard to say.

The first time through the canyon they had nearly been run off the road by a car on the run. His father hadn't taken too kindly to it and had followed them down the winding road, Adel screaming because, of course, Adel liked to be in charge of speed.

Neither of them was afraid of anything as long as they were in control. So, while the old man took the corners so fast the tail end spun around, kissing the guardrails, Adel screamed next to him, nearly in convulsions, and in retrospect why not? She had just lost a son to speed, and she had her remaining five children in the back seat. But he didn't stop, never did stop for anyone. He would have chased them down himself if he could have got away with it, and likely given them a good beating too. He was still young then, and awesome to look at. When they caught up with the car, the bandits were coming out of a trading post, arms full of pelts and shooting in the air. They all watched in disbelief as the bandits got back in the car and drove on – stupidly, as Jean pointed out, because they were headed into a road that would end in a roadblock. There was only one way out of the canyon. And when they did come upon the scene, there were several police cars and the stolen car in the middle of the highway. Turns out they were armed bank robbers, wanted in three states and two provinces. The old man made the policeman march the driver up to our car window and peer in at us in the back seat, which made Adel even more angry because no doubt our faces were burned in his mind and when he got out would he not exact revenge?

Revenge for what?

No, the old man wasn't afraid of anything. Anything but Adel, that is … In the end he spent a good portion of his time appeasing her, bringing her coffee, cooking, and then hating her for it. Jerry had gone over there once near the end and found his father cowering in a corner, Adel swatting him like she had done Jerry when he was young. She could puff up like a cobra, twice the size of him, and nasty. Sure, there were two sides to things. Still, he has no generosity left for Adel.

He does not go to the canyon; at the last minute he veers east on the Hope-Princeton. It's been years, and when he arrives at the Hope Slide he is surprised by the size of it. Back in 1965 it had buried a young couple on their honeymoon. They were driving a yellow vw, which made it seem more tragic. The stone, having covered the entire road, has all these years later only just been pushed back enough for the new road. Chunks of mountain, boulders upright on the roadside. It was, and still is, chilling. They were always on the lookout for falling rock as they drove through the mountains. Always on alert.

He and Guddy didn't bother asking to stop in the slide area: Adel was always making time, making distance … a hundred, a hundred and ten miles an hour in the Chrysler, chain-smoking with all the windows rolled up. In her world the only good reason to stop was a bingo game, a tank of gas or one of her asthma attacks.

But who is he to talk, he rarely stops either. So, stubbing a cigarette into the ashtray, he parks next to a blue van out of which a young boy pops, without a coat, and slips down the embankment into the slide area. Jerry's surprised to find there is a large restroom and a plaque. Several cars parked in front of it, covered with dirty snow. 'Might as well stretch our legs,' he says, pulling on his down vest.

There is something awesome about the amount of rock, how it forced engineers to rebuild the road around it. You think of mountains as still things, but here was one that had moved from one side of the valley to the other. Forty-six million cubic metres over a swath three kilometres wide. Those in their vehicles didn't stand a chance. It's good to remember the power of the earth, he thinks, it's more than something merely sold and trod on. It has a will of its own. It moves. Slowly, most of the time, but then all in a burst like this.

Darlene is standing next to the plaque, scrunching her shoulders up to her ears. He is not a plaque reader, but he is feeling leisurely; the pinch in his shoulder blades has dulled momentarily and he flexes his shoulders. A tour bus opens and a noisy mass of grey bubbles out and around the plaque. In the past few years his hair has completely greyed. For a while he had tried hair products, but he had given in, finally, and felt it a relief. He wonders if Therese and Guddy are greying too, and Bjarne.

'What are you thinking?' Darlene asks

'I'm thinking that this is a lot of rock.'

The boy from the van scrambles around the rocks. He imagines Guddy is still out there doing that, scrambling around the buildings of New York, out at night, at the edge, seeing how far she can go, always discovering something. Maybe she walked up walls? Leapt from rooftop to rooftop? Burrowed under the subway? Once they had dug under a concession stand in a park just after Labour Day weekend; the place was stocked solid with chips and sodas, candy bars and gum. They finally got caught when they started turning in empties by the wagonload.

His own son had not seemed so adventurous, had largely stuck to the yard, taken with his Transformers and Mutant Ninja Turtles. He's making up for that now.

Where would he find the money to help? Did he want to help? Should he help? Could he? Did he even know what was really going on, what he was involved with?

He sees the boy again, running now, from one end of the parking lot to the other, touching the hoods of cars, tears streaming down his face.

Jerry grabs his shoulder as he passes. 'What's going on?'

'My mother,' he says, tears and snot on his face.

'Where is she?'

He shakes his head.

'Where's the car?' Jerry asks this, but he knows immediately what happened.

'We stopped to go to pee.'

'Well, she wouldn't leave you,' he says, 'not intentionally.' He is transported back to Winnipeg, he and Guddy fitting themselves neatly under the underpass, vibrating with the hum of arterial routes, close to an exit ramp, waiting for the car to come back. Trying to make themselves invisible. Thinking they didn't need her, and then worried she wouldn't come. She would leave. She did leave. And so they had to be careful. They had to try not to be a bother because Adel was crying, Adel was sad, Adel was overcome with grief and anger and had kicked them out of the car and driven off.

'Where were you going?'

'To our grandma's house.'

'And where is that?'

'I don't know. I've never been.'

'Where are you from?'

'I don't know.'

'Of course you know. Where did you come from? Where is home?'

'We don't have a home. We sleep in the van. We've been sleeping in it since Christmas. We were in California and Nevada and now we are going to our grandmother's house.'

He is thinking as fast as he can, one hand bracing the boy. He has never understood one thing becoming another the way they did with Adel, and Guddy, but now time seems to be binding different versions of himself. He tries to focus on what's happening now, but what he is thinking of is how much he would have liked his own father to hold his shoulders like this.

Sharp angles come at him, stairwells, under bridges, warm socks, the view from the back seat of the Chrysler. There is the fact of the moment, and then the undoing. There is a tremendous pain in his side, under his left shoulder blade, in the side of his neck. Darlene appears as if she too is bobbing, clinging to a life ring, and then disappears. Everything appears clouded over, and now the voices like fish heading upriver, so many he could walk across the creek, or so they thought, he and Bjarne, that many voices. But this is indulgent, he realizes, and snaps back to the moment.

'Where were you last? What colour is the van? What kind of van?'

'Blue,' the kid says, and that is all he is going to get out of him. Blue. Coming from the coast, he would guess, and then he sees it, clean, which means it's heading into the mountains and snow, not coming out of them. He leaves the boy and Darlene because it seems the right thing to do. He jumps into the Jimmy, pointing it east onto the highway. He will be climbing up to Allison Pass and into snow. She can't be more than ten, fifteen minutes ahead. It's a weekday and thankfully not a holiday, so there are very few people on the road, but the roads are wet.

What is it with mothers running off, thinking a vehicle can be home? Thinking what? That they'll find some new man who will be a sharper version of the last? Why do women still rely on men? Why aren't they self-sufficient? At least, he thinks, and he can't believe he is thinking it, but at least Adel wasn't passive. How many times had they gone off in the middle of winter looking for his father? Would they have been fed if it had been left only to their father? Would he have made better decisions than she? Had he ever gone out of his way to ease them? It was confusing. On the one hand, his father was miraculous, on the other, wholly absent.

He had been on the Hope-Princeton once with his father. Jerry was fourteen and wanted so badly to impress him. They were in the truck, he at the door, Guddy in the middle. He took them not to the fair in Princeton as he was supposed to, but out onto the highway to see a bridge. Not far from here. His father wanted him to think about the construction. Why at this angle? Why with this material? Could it have been designed better? How? But he didn't know. Couldn't answer, and his father went on answering as he asked, talking to himself.

When he walked around a job site his father was always stopping, his head cocked. *Hear that uneven drop? Hear that belt straining? Does it sound like a bulge? Is it tight?* And he was inventive, designing sensors to detect power overloads, circuit breakers, whatever, he just looked and could see the strengths, the weaknesses. But Jerry couldn't hear or see whatever it was his father wanted him to see. So he took a cigarette out of the pack of Rothmans he had in stuffed in his socks and when he was sure his father was watching he took a cigarette out and flipped it from the palm of his hand into his mouth. He had practised for weeks until he had it right.

'What do you think you are doing?'

'Smoking,' he said, striking the match with one hand, another trick he had learned.

'You think you're a big shot?'

Kind of, he thought, but probably didn't say that.

'Who said you could smoke?'

'Who are you to tell me what to do?'

It snapped out of him, a reflex, and his father's hand flew across the cab and hit him square in the jaw. He swiped again, one hand on the wheel, the other batting the crumpled cigarette from Jerry's mouth.

'Fuck you,' Jerry yelled, and the pickup screeched to a stop on the soft gravel shoulder. 'What did you say?' His father out and around to his side, and before he knew what hit him he was out and down, his father pummelling him.

'What did you say?' He remembered looking into the deep crevice below and thinking, Just let me roll down there, into that unnamed creek, who the fuck would care? Then Guddy yelling at his father to stop. And he did.

His father shook him by the scruff of his neck one last time and then let him slump against the cement guardrail. He stared at him for a minute until the dust settled and then he ordered him back in, but Jerry wouldn't move. His father got back in the pickup and screeched off. Of course. Always the screeching off.

Finally Jerry sees the blue van heading into the deep curve that spins both down and around before heading straight up. They are getting near the summit, and snow. There had been an accident on the bridge once. It was summer, he and Adel and Guddy were heading up to the Kootenays. The traffic was stopped. Backed up for miles. A semi-trailer jackknifed blocking the entire bridge. It took hours to clear. People from the town ahead came and sold sandwiches and Cokes out of coolers. He and Guddy lay on the roof of the car long into the night. It felt as though they were at a drive-in. Even Adel gave in to the evening. Lying on the front seat of the car with the door open.

But it's not summer now. The van is travelling fast and he doesn't want to spook her so he waits until they are on a straight stretch and comes up beside her. She sees him and speeds up. He can tell she has told the other boys to strap themselves in and given the van the gas. Jerry pulls back, unsure what to do. He doesn't want to start a chase. He slows down, keeps pace a distance behind her, then turns on his flashers and slowly pulls up and around again. By now the other kids in the back have likely realized one of them is missing. Finally she slows down and pulls over. When he gets to the driver's side, she rolls the window down.

'Do you know where your son is?'

She falls against him and he holds her there, on the side of the road, long enough for her to gain her composure. 'It's okay,' he tells her, 'my wife is at the rest stop with him. He's fine.'

She's sobbing into his shoulder though. Heaving. It was the way his mother reacted to the many rounds of bad news too: the head-on collisions, the trucks spinning off the road, the time his father caught fire, the steel oil rig falling on his head, the not-so-near misses – she just kept throwing herself forward, dragging them along.

'Where is your father?' he asks one of the two boys peering out at him.

He shrugs his shoulders. 'Gone.'

There is nothing more to do here and he is impatient, wanting suddenly to get back home. Thinking now that he would like to get Guddy's call. Go into the city and see her. He would like to see her. He helps the woman back into the van and watches as she turns around and heads back to the slide area. He will do the same. But just for a moment he feels like standing on the side of the road. It's bracing, the emptiness, the way the road drops off. The sun burning valiantly through and making one patch of the mountain seem covered in maple syrup.

His father had hit him so hard that day he dislocated his jaw, and he had to suck his meals for weeks after. His mother had knocked his father in the jaw when they returned. How dare he hit her son? She hadn't spoken to him for weeks, and then there were more roads, more back and forth, more scenes in the car.

He doesn't know his sister Therese, he thinks. He didn't know his father. Why had it always been his mother driving? Why were women always chasing their men away? Why were the men leaving? He pulls out his cell, but there is no service. He is standing in a dead zone.

The room is dark. He doesn't want to go in, but his sisters push him. He sees his mother, in the corner, sweating, heaving. He wants to be near her, tries to scramble into the bed and is dealt with harshly. Torn away again. Then there is a baby crying, and moments after that the wailing stench of death. He will never forgive this baby.

Nor will he justify himself ever again. He is a boy who had his mother taken from him. He is a child of his sisters, and as much as they doted, all six of them, on him, he has been abandoned. He is golden, special, standing tall on a horse as he rides through town. Riding his bicycle over the high, thin arc of the bridge. Climbing sheer rock walls with nothing but his bare toes and fingers. Scaling the church wall. Hanging from the steeple. Defying gravity at every turn. As if he had

suction cups on his hands and feet. Agile as a cat, his sisters said, able to calculate the angles of the world, and look elegant while he did so, and he took pride in this.

How shocking to move from centre stage to a world that saw him as ordinary. His potential snuffed out by a six-pack of children and a wife who thought herself equal. He had never in his life been thought of as ordinary, as equal.

Why leave childhood when it is what soothes? Why not stay where you are the centre of the world? Where all eyes are on you, where the mark of death so early hangs like a halo over one's head and says, Take care of our little one, he has already suffered loss.

And suffering is what distinguishes the adult from the child. The child should not know suffering.

JEAN

He has been walking all night, and tired, he sits on a bench. He puts his paper bag beside him. Water drips down a rocky outcrop behind his head. Bits of moss and plants grow sideways on it. Ships form a jagged line on the horizon. The air so fresh it's like biting into an apple still hanging from the tree, he thinks, like being seven, on a late summer morning. The bench is wet, but he pays no mind to that.

Life is so fleeting, he thinks. Everything is loss. Even an apple. It has to be picked. It's useless if whole. Or it's a piece of art, his daughter might say. He wouldn't. Art is fine for the rich. He has never been rich. For the workingman, any hour not spent working is an hour wasted. You are always on the clock. Each day a deficit.

Come to think of it, why is he sitting here? Here on this bench, people passing, the air, the light, somewhere an old man singing off-key, persistent as the waves lashing at the seawall. On a bad day every sound he hears is his wife calling his name. Other times it is his daughter calling. Either way, he does not want to hear them. The two women who stared at him most intently. Who expected something of him.

On a good day the air is birdsong and the shrill notes of earth slowly shifting. Of the earth he expects nothing, and he is enjoying this moment in his life where no one, save the occasional calling from wife and daughter, expects anything of him. He is not good with expectations. He remembers being taken in to his mother's deathbed by Blanche, or Marie more likely. He had been warned to be a good boy. Not to fuss. He had never been in the room before, though he would inhabit it later, with his father. It was at the back of the house, and dark, cave-like, with something blue, a lithograph of the Virgin Mary on the wall most likely. He was terrified of her face, the last dying ember. Anger rose up in him and he lashed out at her. What had he done wrong? Why was he being punished? He was led from the room kicking and screaming – he hadn't seen his mother in weeks and he wanted her to notice him, hold him. Later, the sounds of a baby crying. The baby, Marie-Agnès, like a sausage in his sisters' hands, was the death of his mother. He tried to put his foot in his new sister's face. He poked at her. Put a pillow on her mouth. They couldn't be left alone in the same room.

Now he is filled with regret. He thinks of Marie-Agnès, whom he has never visited, in her house in the suburbs of Paris. She became a feminist. Only a few years between them, but it was as if they came from different eras. Therese had kept in touch, of course. The angry women bonding. His own anger flares. He feels himself drifting and turns to grab the bench, fastening the rope he looped around his pants to the bench and sitting back down. When he isn't paying attention he sometimes floats off and finds himself places he does not want to be. He is still learning how to manipulate his situation.

Though where exactly does he want to be? He cannot recall and this is frustrating. He should be working, but he cannot find the job site. He has lost many ideas, many thoughts, many things. His old blue work van, for one. He gets so exhausted things seem to fall away. Now he has only his paper bag. He isn't about to let that go. Not yet.

At low tide he watches a family walk out on the green rocks and poke at tidal pools, all of them crouching down to peer in. When the tide goes out there are long flat stretches of rock covered with some kind of green algae. Birds pluck mussels from the pools, fly high and drop them on the rock to break them open. People come and prod, kayakers float past. It really is miraculous and he keeps wishing he had a camera to record it. Later, at high tide, a seal pokes his head up as if he were going to climb up the stairs onto the walkway. He can see the seal's eyelashes, and in his eye, the city reflected like a fish-eye postcard, something Therese would have sent him.

A group of men, Korean perhaps, arrived with buckets and lines and sat on tiny stools smoking, talking, occasionally pulling up what looked to be a kitchen strainer filled with small fish. They enjoyed each other's company immensely, he could tell, and it made him homesick.

There are the runners, solitary or in pairs, dressed in tight clothing. The women with beautifully designed strollers, the dog people, the regulars who come to sift the beaches with metal detectors, the ones who walk along the water's edge searching for things washed up. He has been here before, to this spot, though he can't remember why or when. There is something here for him. Some reason, yes, that he keeps coming back.

He spent the better part of the previous week at the airport, walking along the dike, staring up at the planes. He still recognizes the designs and features. Still likes watching the landing gear drop down, the glide in, as much as he liked the taking off. It's thrilling, the ascent. Thrilling the way the air holds the belly of the plane. It's not any one movement that appeals, it's movement itself, it's remembering the drift of wings, how with one touch the plane veers to the left or right. Like having steel skin.

He spent a night in a field of horses, another in a culvert, another on a reservation he didn't even know existed, another on a golf course, several walking through massive, silent estates, another watching the steady razing and flattening of a field for what he assumed would be a parking lot, or a big-box store. He doesn't go to the place he lived with his wife. He hasn't forgotten Adel. He wishes he could. He hasn't forgotten his children. He wishes he could. His daughter Therese calls for him. His wife calls for him. He no longer wants to hear.

He walked to Mitchell Island where he once worked, and found that the men whose company he had once enjoyed were incapable now of hearing him, or seeing him. He slept in an old dump truck for a few nights. He woke to dogs eating something that looked like a small cat. He woke to men dumping a body in a construction site. He sat on a log boom. Something he had always wanted to do. It wasn't very exciting. In the morning he saw fish breaking the surface of the river.

He likes fish, and fishing, the idea of it, catching, killing and eating. It makes a man aware of the trade-off: one body for another. Life is so material. Matter changing shape. Bodies exchanging forms of energy. The delicate can afford wide swaths between appetite and implication. He preferred to know. Once, on the Skeena, he landed a thirty-five-pound chinook. It was like wrestling a man, how it pulled at the current and dragged him in up to his hips. He was so filled with respect he wanted to cut the line, but then he thought, no, the more respectful thing is to finish it. Earth is the dominion of man, his bounty, and all that. He wanted to touch that fish, to slice into the flesh the way his sisters had slit the necks of chickens and pigs, hung ribs in the cellar, cured ham, the way his brothers could take down a wild boar.

The further we walk away from our food, the sadder we become: this is what he believes. Thinking that death is something you can avoid is even worse. Getting one's hands on death, feeling life drain, this is an essential experience. Sleeping over what will eventually feed you. Their own food in bales, providing your warmth. Knowing that it costs to be human. That your life is taking from the world, and that you need not take too much.

The rabbit stew his sister made back in the days when they had 'so little.' So little made his mouth water. So little with its pure tastes. So little mixed with air, with fresh water, with the smell of stone, lavender, blood. So little was a matter of invention. A matter of perspective. All his life he thought of himself as having little. But was that ever true? Had he ever known little? In this country, in this winter, a man might say he had little, though he doubted the veracity of such a statement even here. In a tent in the tundra relying on food shipped in, yes, that was precarious, but it still wasn't little. At the mercy of weather, yes, but not little. Challenged, sure, but not little. He came from a people who survived thirty-foot snowfalls, who made small republics of their domestic lives. He had failed at this himself. He had failed miserably. He both romanticized his life and loathed it. He both loved his family and loathed the weight of it. Even now, when he can sense his daughter needs him, he cannot find his way to her.

A helicopter hovers down along the seawall like a dragonfly before lifting off up and over to the north shore, giving him the sensation of being watched, though he knows that isn't true: no one can see him or hear him. He can effect no change, only witness it.

The peaks are covered in snow already – or still: the seasons are hard to distinguish. The houses have inched, he notices, especially in West Vancouver, far too high up the slope. It's a town, a province, difficult to rein in. They've endured so many awful politicians, and now a premier who would sell his mother for a profit. Too much development, too little thought. Too little planning. There will be mudslides. They will not have taken erosion into account. They will not have studied rainfalls and slide histories – not to the extent they should have. These people have a strange notion of time – as if things began the moment they set their minds to them. They don't have the benefit, as his people do, of knowing that the Roman Empire invaded their lands a few thousand years ago and stuck their ancestors' heads on spikes. They don't fear invasion of any kind, and so, even as it seeps into their skins, they don't see it coming. They don't understand how to defend not only against invaders but snowfalls, erosion, avalanche, drought, fire. They're like the Overlanders, heading down the Fraser on a raft thinking they're on the Thames.

He realizes, with some surprise, that he is shoeless and it is cold. People pass him in layers of fleece, on foot, in buggies, on bicycles, even in kayaks and canoes, with hats and scarves. The layers seem to have appeared suddenly. Moments ago there were shorts and T-shirts, he is sure of this. Now it is cold. How long has he been sitting here? No matter. In the air force he walked across hot coals and glass shards; as a child he walked over ice, rock, all barefoot. He believes, has always believed, in preparing for the worst. He does not believe that preparing oneself for the worst makes the worst happen; that kind of superstition is his wife's province and he does not want to think of her. No. So he goes back to the beginning as if he were fingering beads, and in the beginning was loss, yes, loss.

Loss, and with loss a preparation. Of sorts, he thinks, certainly of sorts: his mother, soon after the silent sister, then his aunt Maloune, and when her face appears he lights up. His aunt Maloune, and then his sisters Blanche and Lolotte, who doted on him, who were such full beings, as well-read as they were down-to-earth. He aches to see them again. He aches to hear their voices, to sit in Maloune's garden and hear her laugh. He keeps going back, thinking if he can start at the beginning and walk through, in a straight line, walk through his life in an orderly, logical manner as he used to ascend the mountain behind the house of his youth. But no, he is constantly distracted. Now the sound of water falling down the side of the rock behind him is barely audible with waves crashing a little more enthusiastically than earlier in the day. Nowhere, he thinks, not even this place, is more beautiful than his valley. And in that valley, nothing more beautiful than rock, which after all must be the real beginning, the foundation of the earth, soil collecting in its crevices, inching up the sides of its shale and granite. Underfoot, above, shortening the days, sawing off the sun early in the day, building his legs and arms, his heart, a palette of grey, purple, grey.

Rock and life pooling on it, leeching into the most ungiving of substances.

In the fall: hunting wild boar.

In the winter: snow, hot wine, snow.

In the spring: marmots, crocus.

In the summer: garden, field, killing vipers with a forked stick, digging rock.

In the beginning: rocks, and without knowing it, a taste for them. Those rocks that later he would crush, would know what drainage to expect, what grade, what diameter, what texture, how big a slice of mountain per kilometre of road. He picks up his paper bag. Inside are six rocks, of perfect proportions. They have no individual significance, but as a unit they mean something to him. He sets the bag down again, closer to his hip.

Two men appear. Orange reflective vests. Park or city employees. Typical workingmen: loud, chattering, like empty metal things rolling along the pavement; hands fat, delicate as baseball gloves, heads thick and hollow. He's exaggerating, yes, but only slightly. The men are the same height, one a bit heavier, blond, flushed cheeks, standing around as union men will do, smoking, taking their time. Neither stops to take in the view, neither is aware of him there on the bench. All the better for him, as he doesn't want to have to speak, his mind drifting back to the men in the village, those long summer nights after working the fields, the line of them pissing into his sisters' geraniums. They were not a lazy people. There was pride in work. He could not fathom the empty souls of men who took no pride in their work.

He listens to their talk. It's always the same, the empty stories, or what he used to think was empty. He sees the men knitting something as they talk. Something like a net between them. It is soft, worn in parts, but quite durable, quite tangible. He has noticed this and it surprises him. It seems so feminine, and yet not. And the men, gruff as they look, have a softness to them. He had had little patience for his crews. They filled his head with chatter about women and sports, sports and women; minds with little give, thin, easily rotted, or snapped. A few of the men were dogged, always asking him questions. He had not been flattered.

The men are here because they have to replace part of the seawall that was washed away. Now we'll see what they're about, he thinks. We'll see if they've a brain to set to actual work, or whether they'll lean on the spade and wait for instruction. The sun sets. Rises. Sets. Tide goes in, out, in. The men come again. They putter and jab. They are putting in time, and so Jean has no interest in them. Water splashes over the wall. A skunk arrives, waddles off. He is thinking of resistance. All of his life he resisted: and why? He shifts his feet; that's the extent of it. Mind flits, mind flits. He thinks of the whore's room in Paris where he took his bride, unknowingly of course. He thinks of his aunts in Marseilles, the colour of their parlour, the thin mattress they laid out for him in the linen closet when he stayed. How sad they looked when he presented his wife. How in her they seemed to see the end of him. They knew she would never stay in France. He had assumed too much.

He is thinking of all the jobs he has had, the houses he has bought and lost. He started out delivering coal, and then limestone. He started elsewhere as an engineering clerk in the research and development department. He was learning, not earning, and he drove cab at night while his children slept. They went to Vancouver for part of '54 and '55, bought a house on 12th, just east of Fraser, but he lost that when he knocked down the wrong house in the west end. It wasn't necessarily the wrong house, it would eventually come down too, but not that day, and he was responsible. There were so many houses to be knocked down so that high-rises and apartment buildings could go up in their place that he easily won bids, and just as easily lost it all.

Stay, his brother-in-law said, Vancouver is booming, get a stable job, just dig in, pay the legal fees, you'll recover, have your house back in no time. But Jean heard the clink of the cell door behind him. No thanks. He was not up to a nine-to-five life, commuting to and from Surrey or Delta, playing touch football on Sundays. So wipe the slate clean by scurrying out of town in the middle of the night with things loaded down on the roof and five kids crammed in the back seat, and head west to Alberta. Oil boom. Give it a try? Why not Though he hated the prairies, at this point they could not afford to be picky. Then 1956, the oil fields, Wellex drilling: not quite the great money he'd heard about, and his wife having to work in a bar serving his comrades beer and emptying ashtrays. Then, out of nowhere, several hundred pounds of steel on his head. Months of hospital to follow. Where was the oil company? They wanted to settle, but he had nothing to settle. He would take money from no man.

It was retribution, Adel said, for running out on his troubles in Vancouver. The developers had tried to recoup the money from her brothers-in-law and they were not impressed. Well, nor was he, having barely survived. She ran back to Winnipeg, to family. Who else would care for her? He certainly could not. The idea came then. Maybe times had changed for him too? Maybe he could walk away. Send money back. Men did that. He was not cut out for fatherhood. He lay there thinking terrible things, that God was punishing him for his procreation. His wife's cousin had gone mad when his wife gave birth to a child with cerebral palsy; they had found him down on Hastings Street trying to tear off his penis.

What is a man? What is a father? What is a family? Who is at the wheel? Who is driving his future? That is what he thought about those months in traction, those months willing himself to walk. And he did. He took the bus to Winnipeg. He was prepared to do whatever he needed to do to make amends. Until he saw her, the kids grabbing at his thighs, yet another of his brothers-in-law, in soft shoes, carrying in bags of groceries. He would not become a man who wore slippers and carried in bags of groceries. He would not become a man who cooked dinner and chased after children. The thought repulsed him. He was not an indoor man. He was not a city man. He should have stayed in the air force. He should be flying planes right now. He had enormous wingspan. He felt himself bumping and bumping against the walls, suffocating. 'Walk with me,' he said to his wife, and she did, to the newly cleared patch of land that would be a strip mall on Grant Avenue. 'I don't want to be married anymore,' he said, and she said calmly, and to his great surprise, 'Fine. I will be fine without you, Jean. Easier to live with my own regrets than yours.'

He walked down Grant feeling like a new man, like he had his whole life ahead of him. Free. He could wipe away those mistakes and start fresh. He would buy a truck. He would drive back to British Columbia. He would find a job in the Interior, build a cabin on the side of a mountain. He would grow sweet peas in the summer, when he was home, and he would hunt deer and prepare his own food. He would send money. He would support them from a distance. He would be responsible. Better yet, he would go back to France and work with his brothers. He would have his own house. He walked all the way to the Fort Garry Hotel thinking of all the things he would do. Start big, he thought for some reason. He went inside, to the cool lobby, in his work clothes, which was, he realized, all he had. The clothes on his back.

What was he thinking? A broken man of twenty-something could not run to some mountain cabin, nor back to the air force, or back to the valley, or back in time. His father was gone. His brothers had taken the reins in his family. Where were his reins? Where was his future? What would his children do? Who would care for his wife?

'You had a choice,' his sister Blanche had said once, when he was whining, wanting to come home. 'Now your only choice is how you remain.'

He did not love the land for what it was. No, he hated it: the whole damp, flood-prone province of Manitoba. He didn't love his wife for who she was, even though it was what attracted him to her: her vitality, her in-your-faceness, her wilful individuality, her legs and arms, her beautiful neck, her cleavage, the way her calves looked when she stood at attention. Other women paled in comparison. Other women had no edges. No shape. He had been yoked by beauty, by a sublime ability to make him bent over with desire. And he paid whatever price. Whatever price, to stay. He wanted to kill the very thing he was drawn to. Wanted her to be like Maria Chapdelaine, a strong woman who could help him push back the crust of muskeg and create a campfire. He thought of her under the northern lights. Jack pine and spruce, miles of it. It would be different. He would keep her indoors, away from the beer parlours and men who drooled and swatted, from the dancing and shuffleboard. He would force her to learn the domestic arts. He would do so in a positive way, through encouragement. And then she arrived, the first woman in Thompson, under the *click, click* of cameras. What would she find? How would she fit in? Everyone said six months, five months, two months, a week? She was who she was, why couldn't he see that?

One look and you could see. Sculpted calves and arms, shoulders meant to be laid bare. Her hair was thick and waved like a movie star. She had more poise than anyone he had seen off the screen, her ankles always in heels, her delicate feet pointed, like a dancer's. It was crushing to live long enough to despise the very thing you have devoted your life to.

There were a few moments of peace. He could smell them still, the meals, her perfume, hear her heels on the hardwood floors. The way the blue plastic dinner plates slid on the tabletop, how the knives scraped. How well she cooked in the early days. The pies, the cakes, the roasts. Being a good provider. Buying her a wringer washing machine. Eating in the orange kitchen because their bedroom was in the dining room. A meatloaf with Campbell's soup. How clean the house was, how the children smelled after their baths, lined up from big to small in the living room to say good night.

But there were more fights than peace. There was her inability to stay put. The running away, as she finally did, leaving their house in Thompson empty, and then they were back in Winnipeg, and he going back and forth to find work, and then there was his son Joe heading out one early November evening.

At fifteen his son already towered over him, his hair combed to the side like Jean's was. So tall. Jean was sleeping on the sofa half listening to the news and the bustle of dishes being washed in the kitchen. The sort of blissful moment a man agrees to marry for. Stretched out with a family around him. Suddenly she's all over him, wanting him to say no, then when he does say yes, when he wins, she's wanting him to be forceful about a curfew. Joe would have to be home by eleven.

'Woman. He's practically a man,' he had said, and slipped Joe a five-dollar bill: *Take her out for a hamburger*, knowing look, squeezing his shoulder, the first time a child of his was going off on a date to a dance. It felt like such a monumentally common gesture, as if he too were now passing a test, his son a man, and he the father of a grown man. The two of them standing at the door, his son a thinner image of himself, waving him off, waving off the overly protective mother, enjoy, relax, enjoy, relax, and he had gone back to the sofa.

But of course Joe did not come home. Instead the police came, and then he drove to the hospital. It was very cold and Adel was beside him, inconsolable.

His son in critical condition. His son in a coma. His son had catapulted out the window, that's the word they used, *catapulted*. Slammed headfirst into a telephone pole. Jean and Adel emerged from the Valiant, dazed, as if drunk, bumping against each other as they rushed into the hospital; the corridors seemed filled with sludge and they pushed against it, heads down. He held Adel's arm, but she broke away, banged against the walls, willing herself into his room, where she lunged at him. The nurses tried to restrain her. There was blue light from somewhere. A metallic taste in his mouth. He saw his son's head wrapped in gauze. Catapulted out of the car, he kept thinking. Right through the windshield. Terrific speed. Head on. There was extensive damage. Left hemisphere. Internal bleeding. They couldn't know how much.

He was there when his mother died, when his sister Juliet died. Nothing prepared him for this moment.

It's not time, he thinks, leaning over the coffin before him. His son's face hardened into the barest hint of a smile, his thin tie and blue cardigan pinned tightly to his chest. His daughter Therese is there, touching his shoulder, willing him to feel her intensity. Her dark eyes burning like two hot coals in snow. She stands like a Roman column, Annie too, his sons flanking like small, taut lions. The young Therese, not the puffy Therese he had seen riding an electric bike along the seawall. This Therese holds his elbow. They look into the coffin at Joe. Jean smells geraniums. Feels stone crumble underfoot.

We have a home in another time, he imagines telling them, this isn't our real life. One day we'll pack up ... Though of course he had not done that, never done that, never let them know they had a home they could go to, or a language that was theirs, or a history. He touched his son's black hair, smoothed to one side, never again to fall across his brow.

'Jean!' He turns, but it is not his sister, it is his mother-in-law. 'What have you done?'

'I have no idea.'

'You never have any idea,' she says.

That is true, he notes. He can hear her judging him and it sounds like water beetles.

Still, his mother-in-law, whom he sees as having horns on her head and a metal vest, a sword always raised just above his head, had come through. She had arrived for the funeral. For her daughter. She was the only one who came. Death terrified his wife's family. It terrified his as well, apparently, or perhaps just the transatlantic flight terrified them. In any case, only Adel's mother appeared. Even that wasn't enough to hold Adel, however, and he watched as grief pulled her out to sea, the remaining siblings bobbing along in the shallows.

His mother-in-law had a heart of ice. She had cowed her own husband to death, so far as he could tell. Just before Joe's first birthday, she found him hanging from the light fixture in their bedroom in the North End of Winnipeg.

A heart of ice was not precisely true. She had warmth under the surface, but her anger was precise. She had a way of soldering through his chest. She did not have any way of soothing. He wants to hang his head and let her take a final blow, he wants to bury his head in his hands and weep, but he has his other children at his side, by the coffin.

In the folds of satin there is emptiness. Vast. Like sticking your face in glacial water.

The death of a child is a solitary island, he thinks. It is a land inhabited by the sad few.

There is no light that your face doesn't appear in, his sister Blanche liked to say. He thinks he should have said something like this to his son because it has fed him his whole life, that line, her smile; it is utterly sentimental and yet it has been, for him, one very true thing. He didn't want to leave his son, not in a land he detested, and yet he did. He isn't cut out for that kind of cold, for that city, the way it lies exposed in the belly of the arctic wind, too cold, too flooded, too filled with mosquitoes and poverty and booze. Even the good working people fell prey. He wanted to curl up in Blanche's lap. He still does. How is it possible that he is a father? They were good children, they didn't pull, they didn't fuss, they moved with him like particles in water. Still, he wanted to shake them off him. To free himself.

He was the centre of the world. He didn't know how to make anyone else the centre. He didn't know how to share it. He didn't know how to leave it either. He still doesn't.

'I don't know what to do now,' he says to his wife's mother.

'Hold tight,' she says, 'you are floating away.'

He imagines shovelling words into the crusher, dump trucks full of all the useless words he has spoken in his lifetime. He could pave a good section of road with those words. Finally they would be useful. Not that he hasn't been a man of his word, just that his words have done little more than evade.

He is nearly upside down before he realizes it. He rights himself on the bench and in doing so he sees the view from the opposite direction. Suddenly he sees. It is Therese's bench that he is sitting on. She has sent him a dozen photographs of herself from this exact point. Her favourite place in the city. He has seen photos of her standing here in all seasons, in the rain, in the golden hour, in the early light, standing rigid, hand on her breast, staring intently at him across the miles.

'Jean!' She is calling him and he won't answer. 'Jean! I can't breathe. I can't breathe without my puffer. Can you get it in the drawer? Can you just pull the drawer open? Jean, I can't breathe ... and you know Therese is in trouble, Jean, you know, and you know that I know, and you know that I can't breathe, you know and you don't come, and there is something wrong with our baby, Jean. There is something wrong.'

His wife, now so thin she can't quite open the drawer by her bed, calls on him often, but he no longer responds. The drawer, which contains, among other things, containers of Ativan, Clonazepam, Tylenol 3, Combivent, Tums; butterscotch Lifesavers; her teeth; his ashes and his passport; bobby pins; nail clippers; stubs from his pension cheques (now hers); several flavours of Halls; Planters Peanuts; a note, his last to her, scratched hastily on a Visa bill that she refused to pay; hand cream; lottery tickets; baby wipes; pens; prayer card; scraps of paper filled with lists of alphabetized names;

a miniature flashlight; and many other items, common and strange, necessary for his wife to pass the time.

He no longer goes to her and no longer knows if she is where he left her. It doesn't matter where she is, the set-up is the same. He can no longer watch her suffer. She smells like an old woman. She smells mean, acrid, her once beautiful feet now dry, hard, porous as lava, her hands like gardening utensils; her mind honed on vengeance; her neck bent from years in bed; where her belly was, an empty cave. The woman he once worshipped, the woman who kept him leashed with his constant need to touch her, to see her, to feel her skin, now only turned his stomach. At his lowest point, he thought of poisoning her, but she was already poison, and his own hatred had poisoned him. He was ashamed of himself. His indifference had made them both rot. He wishes he had known this in life. He should have walked away. She might have flourished on her own. She deserved to flourish. She deserved to be her best self. She might have at least found peace. But neither of them could cut the knot. Neither of them had the guts to let go.

He had given Therese a camera. He urged her to document everything. She had a great eye. She was a real artist. He sees her now. Just for an instant. Standing by her bike, one hand covering her missing breast, staring at him with such adoration. Then she begins to fade.

Born in the modern city of Winnipeg, his mother came into this world with one hand reaching – was that her childhood? And his father? Born ninth, he fell into his own father's lap in a small hospital in L'Argentière, to a mother who would die bearing the tenth. So it is always the mother we pass through. Always that first opening. The vessel carried, the seed horde and gate, the place he wants to return, always, and would, even now.

He stares and stares at his mother, trying to make sense of the moment of rupture, of the loss, of the cycling through of emotions. It begins here. It begins there. He doesn't need to probe because his mother is always busy keeping everything alive. To his mother the past is a well-loved blanket she must keep airborne always; she must see the pattern of things, and so she too is busy tossing her childhood in the air, examining, looking for thin bits, tears, what needs patching, tending, caressing, where it is soft, worn.

Her arms must be so sore, tossing them all up in the air.

Childhood is that patch. Childhood is the soothing. Childhood is in the air.

He is envious of the blanket, her attention; he is never too old to want her to toss him in the air and stare and stare. He will do what he must to make her look at him, lap him up, soothe with her eyes.

Even more so now that there is a hole in his world. He cannot explain the behaviour, one choice over another, one moment of digging in, one moment of

*letting go, the constant threat of being buried under,
alive. No pattern emerges. He imagines his mother
chained to a sinking ship. They are all swimming away
but she clings, unable to let go:*

My son, *she says*, my son is in that ship.

But he is dead, he is buried, and I am your son too.

He is my son, *she says*, he is my first-born son and
I cannot leave him.

*But they do leave him. At least in body. Though
much of the time he thinks his mother is still there, staring out after the long-lost one.*

I will never cut my hair for you, *he tells his brother,
dead, floating like a slow, steady current above his
head. He could reach out, tap into the field of energy,
zing himself forward, out of the house if he wanted. He
wants nothing but the lap of his childhood. He wants
things the way they were.*

*He watches people strain at the cords, strain and pull
and shred. Consciousness is a harbour filled with
bobbing heads and long, thin anchors.*

*He watches his mother in the mirror. She is getting
ready for an outing. Not a romantic outing as seen in* TV
*childhoods or read about in books. His mother's outings
are to auctions, flea markets, bingo halls, legions, beer
parlours, estate sales, casinos. She dabs foundation
around her eyes and the ball of her nose and smooths,
applies her lipstick only to her top lip, then rubs her lips
together. She does not want to appear garish, she tells
him, punctuating this point with tales of her sisters-in-
law, the nuns and their dismay at her skirts and lipstick:
it's important not to appear overdone, though even then*

he can see that his mother need not do anything to appear overdone; she is simply more woman than others, more curve, more blond (even if it comes in a bottle and is soaped in by his small, gloved hands), more thigh, more skirt, more ankle, more heel, more breast, more slender neck, more cleavage.

Most nights she wraps a scarf around her head, but not tonight. Tonight her hair is freshly dyed, curled and combed. Tonight she wears a red dress with white polka-dot trim. Sleeveless, the skin of her freckled arms gathers like linen, not quite as abundant and soft as his grandmother's, which he likes to hold, when she visits. His mother hums as she sprays her Yardley, smoke encircling them both, and there will never be a more beautiful sight. His uncle has sent her Chanel No. 5, which she keeps in a box on her dresser, and will eventually throw out, or give away unopened. She is not a complicated woman, she likes to say.

Before leaving she takes out her teeth and brushes them in the palm of her hand. In the middle of her pregnancy with Annie, she likes to tell them, she woke in the middle of the night choking on her teeth. Everybody's worst nightmare, but it really happened that way. Annie drained her of calcium and was born with hair so long it curled around her ears and fingernails so long they left scars as she slid out. Some take more than others. You, she says to Therese, even in the womb you were difficult. Or you, she says to him, even in the womb you were sad. You were my good, sad boy.

And the child wants to be good, wants to fit, even as he butts his head, even as his feet flash first through broken glass and tantrums; it is good that he moves toward whatever good is – however far it is from him, that is where he travels.

BJARNE

In the beginning there was shadow. That much he remembers. One brother in the bed beside him, another above, and shadows moving across the wall; long swaths of darkness that came from nowhere and went nowhere and threatened to take him as well.

In the beginning there was his father, walking away. Into the red forest he went and came back with the head of a black bear, the hoof of a red deer, dappled fish squirming in a knot at the end of his fist. In the beginning his father climbing into his blue truck, steel lunch pail banging against his granite thigh. How large he was, like a smokestack, his hands straining like eagles. He could grab anything from the earth, from the air, and hold it in his palm: the hearts of children, the lungs of women, the bark of dogs.

In the beginning there were trees. As far as the eye could see and farther than he could imagine, silent, shivering battalions circling in on him. There were shallow lakes, fast rivers and mosquitoes woolly around his nose. Trucks came and went with gravel and concrete, they came spraying DDT up and down the freshly paved streets. Summer he and Therese played hide-and-seek. They sang together in church and after dinner. Long winters he searched for his mother's lap, away from the colours that moved and changed shape.

In the beginning there was Joe, he thinks, or no, doesn't think, doesn't want to think about the beginning or the end, doesn't want to think about thinking, or even not thinking, five six seven eight ...

In the beginning there was something light, something sweet, something melodic, something gurgling, he thinks, and gurgles himself, gurgles on his cold coffee, gurgles to amuse. Something with bubbles, he thinks, carbonated, and begins rocking.

Eleven, twelve, thirteen ...

In the beginning his father with a six-pack of Cokes. A trip to the park. He can smell the earth, Winnipeg earth, moist, smelling of river, of cottonwoods. Those trees, he thinks, those trees with feet followed him all the way to Terrace. They live now on Ferry Island (or is it Fairy Island?), where the men line up to fish in the summer and where he walked once with his niece and his sister Annie, and he saw faces in the trees. They really are faces, they have been carved in, Annie said, he can't be sure. Doesn't trust Annie to know. They look real. And those cottonwoods. Big as buildings. Thick with crows. The tadpoles were nearly ready, his niece told him. Blackbirds cawed, smacking their wings for dinner.

This is why he doesn't like to go out. The world is dark. Crows line up to eat babies.

His sisters send him shoes, coats, hats, urging him out into the world, but he doesn't budge unless he absolutely must. In here he is in control. In here the only shadow to move is his own.

He does not need daylight. He does not need air. He did enough walking in Vancouver. Up and down Hastings over to the park on Powell. Down Gore to the Missions to Seafarers where, even though he isn't a seaman, he could sometimes get dinner, accompanied by piano even, and hear stories from the sea. Twenty-one, twenty-two, twenty-three. Over to Oppenheimer Park, past Princess, Hawks Street, the seams of the city, ragged.

He sees things. Yes, he sees things. But what does he see?

What he sees is what everyone else sees, only he sees the strings. He sees the strings yearning, the colours travelling along the spindly threads behind objects; he sees dogs with wings, cats with scales, words like icicles hardening in the air before him, tiny fists banging from inside the walls. Other people don't have strings on their thoughts; they don't get tripped up because they don't see the strings. They have a way of thinking that is not stringy. They can keep things separate. He would like to look at something and not see it the way that Annie doesn't see it, or Jerry, or Janine, the nurse at the health unit, who is very nice, who has three kids and lives on a patch of land outside town and has horses, and doesn't see strings but feels compassion. She feels it very aggressively, her desire for good. She would smother him with good intentions. She would not know. She would stuff them down his throat until he choked and she wouldn't know any better. He knows she doesn't know, that she doesn't see, because things are right before both of their eyes and she can't see them. Or she can't see them in multiple ways. It is not exactly a failure to acknowledge. She sees something. She is not stupid.

In any case, he knows more about her life than she does his. If she pieces anything together she doesn't let on. He pieces things together though: photographs on her desk, the notes on her calendar, the phone calls she sometimes takes when he is there. She never assumes he is listening because he has his head down, his hands folded between his thighs, tightly, close so as not to offend, but he is listening. Give me my shot, he thinks. I have nothing to say to you, or you to me. She is doing her part. She is saving him from his mind, she thinks. His schizophrenic mind. He is playing his part to amuse her, to amuse all of them, but it is also practical: if he doesn't take his shot he doesn't get his cheque. So there it is, the compromise.

He wants no trouble. No fighting. No violence. He rolls his fingers back and forth, back and forth, creating another small perfect ball to add to the pile on his night table. If he opens the door and looks out the window in the hall, he can see the train tracks, and in the distance, much closer than Vancouver, the mountains. They are often lost in clouds, but even then you can see the base of them, and the trees individually, and then all together as if they are huddled, looking down at him. But he doesn't open his door to look. He was in a room with a window before but he moved here. He saves twenty dollars a month and he doesn't need to see out. He hears the trees without looking. He senses them rubbing up against each other. At night he can't imagine how anyone sleeps in the town. The trees are so loud then. He feels his own skin rubbed raw with their longing. Now what would Janine say to that, he thinks.

The trees belong to the natives.

What they want to do with them is their business.

They can stack them. Divide them between tribes and hurl them at each other across the Skeena for all he cares.

One hundred and eighteen, one hundred and nineteen ... rolling, rolling, he doesn't keep track, doesn't keep track of the balls, there is no connection between the balls piling up, and the rolling and the counting. They are what he does. His fingers have to move. His mind has to move. He does care what the natives do with the trees. He does care. He gets angry when he thinks of the natives. How they are cut off from their land. He feels empathy. He feels cut off from himself. He has been logged, he thinks. He has been stripped. He has had every meaningful mineral mined from his soul.

One hundred thirty-eight, one hundred thirty-nine. He can count with his eyes closed. He can count and be aware of his body. Or not. It doesn't matter anymore if he is counting anything. He can feel his feet touching the carpet by the bed. The air from the crack by the door, his elbows, swollen now and aching. He might like a Gravol now. Difficult to get since they started making him give his name. Safeway pharmacy, here to serve, but not him. One hundred sixty-three, one hundred sixty-four ...

The beginning was toffee sweet and a floor shiny as a bowling alley. He smiles at the thought of the floor. Adel kept it so clean, so polished, dragging him and Jerry around on a blanket. He likes the salty, the sweet, the smooth, the pulling,

104

those sweeps of surface glistening, and he and Jerry sliding across it, smashing into walls, he and Jerry, and Joe, who showed them how to slide in the first place, and then just as suddenly seemed not to want to slide, not to have pillow fights, and then *poof*, he was gone.

In the beginning was the mother and in the end he supposes she will be there too, and in the middle, for a moment, there was his big brother and his little brother, and he was a little brother and a big brother. Then no one talked about Joe anymore. His sister Therese and he were pivots, middle children of either gender, embattled. She sends him old photographs, restored, but he doesn't put them up. Doesn't want to look at the past, have those images like crows perched on his walls waiting for the tadpoles to walk out of the soup. In every photo there is a crack down the middle of Joe. A crack splitting him in two, or cutting him out, or a blur where his face was, or a white mark so he can't make him out.

One hundred and ninety-seven, one hundred and ninety-eight …

Next to fade, Therese.

He might need rolling papers today. Might need to go out. Might need to go to his mother's cave, where she has her trophies displayed. Might have Gravol. Will have Ativan. Will have Tylenol 3. Will have ice cream. Will have store-bought cigarettes. He visits her, curls up on one of her furs and licks himself clean. He listens to her talk, brings her tea when she asks. He won't walk there though. Not over the new bridge by Ferry Island with the faces in the trees, not over the old bridge with the gaps between the logs and the river below, where he once saw a bear swimming. No way to evade the big bad wolf. No safe way to get to Grandma's house.

Will have Caramilk bars and Coffee Crisp. Will have chocolate ice cream and nougat. Tins of pudding. Tins of licorice allsorts. Tins of Poppycock and peanut brittle.

Still, not worth walking for. No. Not by the faces. He rarely goes out, and if he rarely goes out, they rarely come in. Banished from his room. He did that. Cast them out. Still, to ward them off he turns up the volume on his television out of habit and Rolf, his neighbour to the left, leaps up to pound the wall, but he quickly turns it down and the movement stops. His hand, Bjarne imagines, poised in the air, like an old Roman or Greek god – how people made offerings to Zeus, to Poseidon, thinking an angry god might smite them or their children, or their children's children? Or closer to home for him, the Norse gods, the bloody battles and sucking of marrow, the *What if God had such a long memory?* That is why there is absolution, because the mind boggles from the strain of all that pain. Can't carry that. Not without sweetener. Or sedative. Or Gravol.

He hears a crow screech past. Something Therese might have said, he thinks, and suddenly he is in quicksand. He knows the feeling. Don't fight it. Don't kick. He arranges his pillows, lights a cigarette, staring now at the door, which he is sure will be knocked on at any moment and when he goes downstairs to take the phone call it will not be good news.

He waits for the feeling to pass. Slightly nauseated. That is how he discovered the pills, or did he get nauseated to take the pill? His problem? Too many feelings. No skin covering his heart. He thinks of a meadow. The one in France the summer he went with his sister Therese. He thinks of walking up the mountain with his aunt who, despite her bad leg, her skirt, the sweater buttoned around her neck, always seemed to be ahead of them, turning back to take a photo. Everything amused her. His hat, his knees, the flowers underfoot, the sun, everything seemed to pop up and say hello. Walking up to the first peak above the small town where his father was born and lived, as so many generations before him had been born and lived, and he thinks of them as rocks, shifting away from the mountainside and walking, together, en masse, across the valley, from one side to the other. He was not afraid then, just aware. Looking down on the past as if it were his. Looking down. Not good.

Down is never good. Down being the dark corners, anything intimate. The whisperings. Not even confession is safe. Not the golden robes, not the silver chalice, not the purple sanctuary. He used to think he wanted to kill the father. He built himself up. Hung from rafters doing chin-ups. Fell to the ground and did push-ups. His stomach was so hard he could feel the response in women passing him on a street. The waitresses who served him. When he took off his shirt his stomach shone like a washboard. Clean. Even the men glanced as they worked. He liked to be clean. He oiled his muscles. Combed his hair constantly. He did push-ups for breakfast. His sister on his back as he did them. He could kick the ceiling. Pin his brother until he squealed like a girl. He could knock anything down, and he did, knocked down doors, smashed windows, pushed the air away, he pumped, and pumped, and then what? What in him? What feeling or thought? What note? What detail hardened there? And one day ... one day what? The father is inside, he realized, inside him ... and then the world started punching through. The bruises appeared. The teeth knocked out. *Come on, fucker, come at me*, and they did, and the punches began to land, and down and down he went.

No. Not that thinking. Not the thought of a body inside him, the essence of a man inside him. He looks up at the tiles in the ceiling of his room and begins to count those. He knows how many, knows each one intimately, but he counts again and he counts again and he counts again. From the beginning, in the beginning, to the beginning, at the beginning, of the beginning ... one, two, three.

There are too many beginnings. Too many wars about beginnings, about origins, about ownership of land, resources, ideas, truth. Someone suggested this to him once – one of the women from the Salvation Army perhaps – that he could give up the war. War is over if you want it to be. War is done. War, as if it were a thing anyone could control. War, as if it were outside.

When he was on the street he often went to the Sally Ann for food, and every now and then they took him out to their camp in the valley. No reason why or when, it seemed to him, random. Or maybe they could see who was nearing the end of their rope and they would give them a little boost, give them strength. They couldn't save, they could only prolong, only try to catch those about to fall and give them enough energy to remain hovering at the edge of the abyss, scrabbling around at the bottom.

He could say the prayers, he didn't mind, though those words got inside too. They made him weep. He tried to hide it, but the badger was stirred. He has to be careful what he lets inside because it worms its way in and the badger wakes, nattering on a loop, its message burrowing into him.

No words. We have no words for Joe. For the one who slipped away. No words he might say, repeating lines he wrote long ago, the only poem: *That last black trek to church, silent. No words, we have no words for the first-born, the brightest star, the one who slipped away, and with him, faith.*

He can give up the war. He can give up thinking, is what she means, but he *has* thinking. Thinking is his. That is who he is. That is what he has. He might not have much, but he has a wheel in his brain going around. Thinking. Some thinking is good. Some is not good. If he thinks of Joe, for example, and then he thinks hair, he will want to pull it out, the hair, that is, which is the opposite of what he wants, which is thinking that soothes because he promised Joe he would never cut his hair and he did, he cuts it all the time. So yes, the words, he thinks, are important. Each word with its associations. He never knows where to put them, the associations. Where do they go? Do people have storage containers full of associations? Is that what is in their houses, their big houses full of stuff? Is that what makes them fat and slow?

This makes him laugh, and he loses track of his count, has to start over. Seventeen, eighteen, nineteen, the numbers become purple and yellow, become blue and swirling, become flowers in a field, become clouds, become cats, have fur, claws, swirl, catch. Words alone, words out of context strangle his brain, pull on his ribs, he coughs things up then, and if he is out, if he is in a restaurant or the mall, he annoys the customers and he has to leave, unless he has gone too far, or is in a mood where he doesn't want to leave, doesn't want to be inconvenienced by their unease, and then he is carried out, or sometimes heaved into an alley by security, or on a stretcher carried by ambulance attendants, or policemen, or strangers who might be kind, or not. Mostly not.

Harvey, the bartender downstairs, knows his limit and Bjarne respects this because he doesn't want to be barred anymore. He wants to walk freely into the bar, which is where he goes when the words lodge themselves. This doesn't happen often anymore with the shots, but still, if they gather strength he can become very agitated. He can become methodically, strangely self-destructive; he knows this, he is forced to know this because everyone reminds him. Illness (which is what they say he is, ill), illness makes you fair game for comment, makes everyone think they should tell you what to do, how to live your life. These are the reasons he will not go to group therapy, he will not sit around with a bunch of medicated men – inebriated men, yes – and at this he

109

laughs out loud: inebriated yes, medicated no.

Rolf bangs on the wall and he raises his fist to bang back but thinks better of it and turns the volume down. He doesn't recall turning it up, but he has. It is loud. Still, he bangs the air for emphasis. War, war, war is apparently what he is. If he thinks about it, the Sally Ann is the only real vacation he has ever had. But the war came with him there, and it came here too. There is no snapping your fingers and ending war, unless that is what death is.

Or maybe death is a vacation.

No. No, it isn't. No, it isn't. And war is over if you want it to be. War is over if you want it to be.

Sometimes he says something to amuse himself and it does not amuse. He lobs an idea in the air and it transforms, its mouth a monster bearing down on him. He rocks, slowly, his eyes closed tightly, twenty-seven, twenty-eight, twenty-nine ...

A crow calls. It sounds like someone choking. That's what Therese would say because Therese also hears things. And sees things. Sees how things are torn apart, can see minute particles in the air reaching out for each other. Saw how Joe became a ghost even before he died. Saw him floating and banging on the ceiling. Saw him walk through the front door at will, tower over their mother and pretend to be pounding her head with a mallet. Small mother go boom, he says. Not a nice thought, but it makes him laugh. He arranges his pillows and lights a cigarette. He is upset at the thought of his mother in pain. He does not want his mother to be hurt. He balances the ashtray on his thigh. His elbow is weirdly swollen. It hurts, which is comforting if not refreshing. For some reason pain is always comforting. If he hurts he is still alive.

'I'm alive! I'm alive!' He pulls his knees together. He has knees. He has knuckles. He has a room. He has cigarettes. He has those chocolate-covered cherries with the juice that runs down his chin when he bites in. He has a lot to be thankful for.

He puts the ashtray aside. Settles in, watching the door. It will be knocked on at any moment. Someone will come up the stairs with a note in hand. Or to call him down to the phone. He won't go. He'll say he isn't well today. He is busy being comforted by pain, he'll say. Or, he's not himself today. Who is he then? He is someone else, he'll say. Who anyone is is so uninteresting, so very uneventful. He won't say this, but he will laugh.

On the other hand, if it's the right tone, or if it's Jessica who knocks, he will have to go down those stairs. He will be forced to because he can't say no to Jessica, even though he is sure it will not be good news. Jessica is transparent. There are no dark corners to be wary of in her. When she walks in, the building seems to squeal with delight. So does he.

He doesn't want to think about the past. There is no good news coming out of the past these days. Was there ever? No, he doesn't think there ever was. Nothing new. No news of the past. No past news. No news past. What he has is now. Another thought he'd best not have. He doesn't believe it. Without the present, can anyone be alive? Without the past? Since he isn't willing to embrace the future and doesn't want to go out into the present, the shadow between the present and the past is where he lives, so best not trouble it too much. Best not stir. Best not dip or straddle, or ride the pot. Best not lurch forward. He and his mother have that in common. They are no longer moving forward. They sit, fat as sea lions. If they lurch, they bump back into each other. They do not swim, they bask. But for them the sun is TV.

Still, he believes his mother would like to move forward more than he would; she would like to get out, she has more will than he, a voracious will to suck up life. As does his sister Therese, who gets out, gets on with things. Keeps moving forward in the face of her illness, which they don't talk about; they don't tell him about it and he doesn't mind not knowing because he knows enough without knowing specifics. He knows as much as the next sibling and he doesn't know how any of them carry on with what they know. He doesn't know why everyone isn't walking around with a broken heart. He doesn't know how everyone is so chipper. So excited about soft drinks. Though he could be excited about a Mama Burger right about now. Or some Timbits. Or a Mama Burger and some Timbits. Or a Mama Burger and some Timbits and a milkshake.

He is closer now to the mountains than he was on Hastings and though he never goes out in them they surround him like they did in his father's town in France. He went with Therese one summer, before he got ill, when they were teenagers, the two of them everywhere together, riding mopeds, hiking up the mountains, and everywhere his father's rays of strength radiated because he was a star in the valley and could do anything: lift a horse, fly a plane, shoot a bird. Now Bjarne is back in the mountains. They surround him like damp fathers, their backs to the campfire, facing out into the night, guns at the ready to protect him. Big guns. Pointed to the sky. He rolls, rocks, adds another ball to the pile of balls, like little ball bearings in the ashtray, like pellets for a gun. There is a gun in his mother's closet. His father's rifle. He doesn't approve of guns. Doesn't like guns. Had one pointed at his head once and yes, he did turn his pockets out, he did do whatever they asked, hit the ground, his chin bleeding, his arm snapped, he kept his head down until the footsteps died away. He didn't want to see their faces.

When they were young, they had rifles. They shot cans and sometimes tomatoes or oranges they would toss in the air.

He enjoyed the feeling of hitting the target, but he never imagined pointing one at anybody.

Though yes. He admits he went to Canadian Tire once to see about bullets for the rifle. He thought about walking into his mother's room and aiming at her head. He thought about it and then he took two fifties from her purse while she was sleeping and went and got very, very drunk. The problem is that someone is always judging his thoughts. Someone is saying, *If you think it, you might as well have done it. You might as well have aimed and shot,* and he does not want to hurt his mother. Never. Never. Never.

Thinking is not doing. Good or bad, thinking is not doing.

He was taken in to a psych ward once after threatening his brother with a shotgun. He held it to his throat. Double barrel. Nostrils flaring. Apparently. He had taken his brother Jerry by the neck and thrown him across the room. He had hit his head on the ceiling, in fact, and twisted his neck. No one knows for sure. One person sees something, starts a story. The story gets embellished. He never held his brother at gunpoint. That never happened.

He gets up and paces the room. His socks like little puppets flopping ahead of him. Six paces by six paces. It was an idea, it wasn't really the way it was, it was an idea of how someone remembered things going, not the reality. He would never point a gun at his brother. That's another matter, and at times this is what comforts him, knowing that memory can be exaggerated. Memory can be telling a lie.

When they finally came for him, he had barricaded himself in his room. He had covered the windows too. You could see too much from the windows, and of course they could see in, the people who were following him, staring at him, saying things, then denying it. Making him feel not right in his mind.

They might have shot through the door. They might have thought he was a deer. He hadn't paid his rent. He wasn't camouflaged. He couldn't take off his skin, no. He hadn't eaten either, hadn't picked up his cheque. So he was lucky nothing dramatic happened. In their family people tended to die dramatically: a cousin was found stabbed in an alley behind Main and Hastings, another was hit by a train, another was decapitated, another had a heart attack at a service station outside Lyon and his cousins had to drive to the Alps with him dead in the passenger seat. His own brother flew through the window of a speeding car that hit a guardrail, his uncle slipped on a patch of ice leaving a bar in Aldergrove and died instantly. This was the uncle that his mother said over and over again Bjarne took after ... That was his future.

That's why he had come up here, to avoid his future.

And when he came up here it was cleaner and people left him alone. Now things were changing. Street life was being pushed out of the city and bleeding outward, into the small towns where it was already festering. It had found its way to the little hotel where he lived next to the train tracks. Used to be alcohol was the big problem here, but now he is surrounded by crack addicts.

But he doesn't have to panhandle anymore, doesn't have to beg for money for something to eat, and other than sometimes borrowing money when he gets his cheque and then not paying him back, his neighbours leave well enough alone. He doesn't have to steal. He could get away with stealing in the city where he could spread his face around. He was good at it. Food mostly. But he can't do that anymore. He only ever did that out of need and now his needs are met. Well, actually, he just can't do it anymore: everyone knows everyone else in town and he doesn't blend in, can't stay under the radar.

If anything, he sticks out. And when he mutters in public, mothers reach out for their children and pull them tight.

The truth is, he could never harm a fly. Not intentionally. Not in his right mind.

He sits on the edge of his bed, aware of the door, of people walking by outside it. He is watching *Judge Judy* and his heart is racing because he knows the woman on the stand does not have the money to pay and he is afraid for a minute that Judge Judy will fail him, that she will, against all odds, make the woman repay the man who is obviously, so very obviously, a charlatan. Just yesterday he watched Judge Judy award a man half of a car that he purchased with his common-law wife. Which half, he thought. How will they do that? He relies on Judge Judy to assert a kind of justice that reassures him. When she fails to do this he takes it personally. As a kind of sign. He is so upset afterward that he has to turn off the TV and go downstairs. There is always a sigh when he walks into the bar, like a spring swell, the river about to spill over its bank, trees all snagged and raucous. Not that the bar is ever full, but he senses that his presence there, the unpredictability of his nature, makes them nervous. 'Bjarne,' Harvey always says, 'how's it hanging?'

The thing about life is its forgiveness, its gentle enfolding; there is always a place for that even when there is no good solution. Even when all the choices are shit. He believes this even in the worst of it. Some ideas are too complex, he thinks, flicking an ash into the small onyx ashtray (yet another gift from Therese). They don't want him smoking in here but he does, and they forgive, they facilitate, and he appreciates. These small things. The accommodation, the way Harvey greets him. There are softer ways of being.

He is thinking of his mother. She had one of those ashtrays that you could make the cigarette ashes disappear into by hitting a plunger. The mechanism spun like a child's top. He could see it working, having taken the top apart and watching the spindle move. He took everything apart to see how it worked and put it together again and after that he could see the inner workings, the axle of the car, the axis, the wheels, the bearings, the inefficient wonder of the internal combustion. As if he had X-ray glasses.

On cold days when they were all forced to stay inside because the wind chill was too dangerous and they were bathed and lined up like ducks in front of the TV, he was squirming. He didn't want to sit in a line, he wanted to be on her lap, but they couldn't all be. He wanted her to himself, but Jerry arrived and took that spot, and then Guddy arrived and took Jerry's spot. He forgave Guddy, he was older then, but he was young when Jerry arrived and he resented him. He imagined walking his little brother to the river and setting him down in it like a twig he could trace the line of as it drifted away.

Somewhere there is a photo of him hiding under the kitchen table, naked. It is warm in the house and he is naked and no one minds. He has the ashtray there, and one hand reaches out to plunge down so the ashes disappear into the cylinder to be seen no more.

No one came looking for him those years on Hastings. Not until the end. He ran into Therese once, and Guddy a few times. They gave him money, took him for lunch. What else were they supposed to do? Take him home? They were all trying to gain some kind of foothold.

Love and let love.

Those days he went back and forth on Hastings, from Main to Cambie, back along Water, sometimes over to Powell. Circle around the park there and come back. But sometimes he went further. Down toward the marina where everything was being dug up and changed. It would no longer be a working port. Not there. Or he went across, into the west end. Over to Davie and down. He never liked the beaches. Never went to the water. He didn't care about the water. Water was for the wealthy. Views were for the wealthy. He didn't care about the views. Didn't like to see far. Wanted to feel enclosed. He slept in hallways. In parking garages. In bathrooms. In shelters. From time to time a friend let him crash in her room in Chinatown. She went away to see her mother up the coast in Alert Bay and then back sometimes in the middle of the night and he was on the sofa, or out if she wasn't alone. The walls hung with rag insulation. The windows were cracked. A poker game had been going on in the room next door for several years running.

You don't belong here, he said to her, and she said the same to him and they had a good laugh because where else were they going to go? He was okay with alcohol. Mixed with Gravol when he could get it. But never street drugs. Never anything in a needle like the zombies that scurried out from under dumpsters and between cracks in buildings and fences and would stab you for a cigarette. Rare for him to walk down the alleys. Never do drugs, never walk down the alleys. Day or night.

Everybody talked about how they got there and none of it meant anything. Laid off. Parents died. Father was a drug addict. Mother a whore. Bullshit. Divorced. Cry me a river. Mentally ill. Bad mind management. Kicked out of the band. Bingo widow. Gambling spoils. Some of them had been sniffing glue since they were children. On the needle by twelve. Even when he was in the worst of it he didn't feel like he was the worst of it. He didn't feel like his mother would sell him for a bit of cash. He was surrounded by people who were treated like bags of wheat exchanged on the market.

He always had one eye on another possibility. He always kept himself neat. His hair combed. They teased him about it. They knocked his front teeth out. But not all of them. He recognized the difference between those who could see a way out and those who could not. Not many came by choice either though. Mostly it seemed to happen very slowly or very suddenly. With him it was suddenly. He had been babysitting for his cousin out in Delta for almost a year while she worked as an accountant and her husband worked at the Liquor Board. He was the overlap and the nanny. He cooked simple meals, watched TV with the kids. They didn't bother him too much, and he mostly remembered to do the tasks his cousin asked. But then he started to forget things. He forgot a pot on the stove and the handle melted before he noticed, he left a cigarette on the coffee table and the three-year-old burned his hand, he fell asleep and burned his mattress, he left the water running in the bathtub and it overflowed, he left the baby in the bathtub once too and returned to find her submerged, but only just covering her ears, thankfully, her tiny arms flailing in the water.

He began to hear voices. He felt afraid of himself. He was seeing things that were both him doing things and things being done to him. He didn't like the feeling, and it seemed directly related to the children. He would be over-come with rage, or with sorrow; he might run, or he might weep. So one day, just after he heard his cousin come in the front door, he slipped out the back. He pretended to have a gun in his pocket and held up a 7-Eleven. It was easy enough. The young kid gave him what he had. Not much, but enough to get a cab downtown, where he stayed for the next five or six years.

When they finally came to pick him up he had apparently locked himself in his room at the Balmoral. He had arrived, he thinks in retrospect, having a room in the Balmoral with a door that locked, a window, a bed. He could barricade himself in. And he did. No one in, no one out. He hadn't eaten for a week when they finally busted through. He weighed just over a hundred pounds.

Then suddenly he was in the hospital. His parents were there. Adel, faithful, but his father – he could see the disgust, the disappointment in his eyes. The way he spoke to him as if he were damaged. It was the worst: his father's eyes.

He slept for months in the joey shack of a trailer his mother bought out in the valley. He saw doctors, he got medication, sounds began to fade, to diminish to a manageable roar. One day he heard birds, clear and sharp outside his window. He opened it a crack and something sweet filled the room. Jerry came by with coffee and they sat in his room. Later Guddy came to plant a garden for Adel. It was Mother's Day. They sat out and had coffee. She said the plant he smelled was called mock orange, and that they bloomed all over the Lower Mainland. Not a native plant, she added, but they did well.

'I'm not a native either,' he said, 'but I do well too.'

After he woke up from Hastings he had enormous forgiveness. He felt full of peace. He was happy to be alive. To have calm. To sit under a tree and watch his baby sister planting things, his father too, with his sweet peas, probing the earth. 'I hope you forgive me,' he had said to her later, over a coffee. 'I do,' Guddy had said, and though he wasn't sure she meant it, he was happy to hear it. 'I forgive you too,' he said. 'I forgive everybody.'

In the beginning is the mother, heartbeat, hands, a lap he needed to constantly curl up in, a palm, a sliver of moon, a bowl of milk soft as a cat's belly. She is everywhere he looks; he would have attached himself to her skirt. He once thought that God came out of there too. He laughs, which makes him rock, which soothes. He would, if he could, crawl back inside. He would undo everything.

Someone is banging on the wall. He doesn't even have the TV on. There is no TV on. So what is he watching then? The clawing starts. It's like an itching in the brain, an itch that can't be scratched, obviously. Little fists, thick with anger. Anger is a marmot-like creature. When the big marmot gets them all going, they start pounding on the walls, all the animals he has eaten: the chickens, cows, pigs, the bison and deer, the coho and tuna, pounding on the walls around him.

On Hastings no one had anything of their own. Whatever you had was the street's. If you looked up and saw the sky you couldn't believe how lucky you were to be there, to have a door that closed, but if he looked down he could see them scurrying on the street. And on the rooftop next door. Once there was a man playing the flute on the roof below, and another time he saw a man slit another man's throat. Nothing surprised him anymore. It seemed there was nothing a person wouldn't do to another person.

Mostly you're on the street and you move with everything you have, daily. You have no reprieve. There is no recharging. No changing. Not a minute to plan your next move. It is constant. You just try to keep your skin intact.

There are men who see you as bricks for their empire. You either fit in or you're pulverized. He slipped through that. He's on the other side. He's just nothing. He's of no use to anyone. The best is not being useful.

Now he feels rich. Jerry calls and checks in on him every other week. His sisters send him care packages. Odd things: sweaters he will never wear, noisy, unflattering jackets with many zippers, goofy fleece hats, shiny T-shirts with tags explaining new technologies of warmth. He used to like his long brown leather jacket. He wore jeans tucked into his Daytons and tight-fitting shirts with wide lapels. He still kept his hair long and shaggy, though now when he looks in the mirror he sees a greying, yellow-skinned man. He sees a thin man in dirty sweatpants, in oversized sweatshirts. He keeps his hair under a ball cap now. He splashes a little Calvin Klein cologne. He has a bank account and a credit card. He can go and suit up at Walmart and have money left over for something in the bar.

Not that he drinks anymore. Well, not often. Not like he once did. He was a champion drinker. He drank and drank until everyone around him was passed out and he was yelling for more.

Women still treat him very nicely. His social worker takes him shopping but he prefers to shop for himself. He lets only women cut his hair. He likes a simple black comb, a fresh comforter and fluffy pillows, a Tim Hortons cup because it's spill-proof. He likes candy bars, smoking, coffee. He doesn't like to read. His sisters send him books, which gather by the window. Eventually he will take them to his mother who reads everything, every surface, every box top and circular that floats by her bed.

He visits his mother regularly. He does his laundry there and loads up on food. He makes her tea and brings it to her in bed. He sits and pretends to listen, nodding until he can't take any more. What he likes best, what they do well together, is watch TV. If she is commenting on *Mindfreak* or *Judge Judy* it doesn't bother him. Mostly he nods, keeps one eye on the window, the mountain there, clouds tickling the top. He nods, giggles approval, and she goes on like a small engine burning off calories. He would like to make his mother levitate. His mother would like to make things disappear. She thinks Criss Angel is attractive. When she talks about this he sends his mind elsewhere.

He should go out there this week. He promised. But he knows something is up. And he is not a man for crisis. Not anymore. Never, actually, though he didn't have a choice for a long time. Or so he thought. *You always have a choice, Bjarne. We all have choice.* His father said that many times but he didn't understand those words until one time he was standing outside his mother's place and he felt calm, and he felt in control: those very words seemed to part the sky, to show him a possible future. *We have a choice.*

But then he started to think about this, about children, for instance: do they have a choice? Can they just walk off? Can they say no? And what about illness? Is that a choice? He is thinking of Therese, who he is sure is not well, and who he is sure he will hear from today, or hear about. He is thinking of how often they found themselves on silent journeys together, the two of them, behind the scenes in the grocery store, or out along the river. The falls in winter with the water shooting under the ice, wearing at it like a tongue. And how, after dinner, the two of them standing tall in the middle of the room singing about Cape Cod girls. He cannot remember the last time he sang.

Once he had a voice. Once he had a car. A Chevy Nova. It was 1977 and he played BTO on his eight-track all the way from Winnipeg to Vancouver with his cousin. The car was gold with a white roof and he thought for a minute that this was how his life would go: freedom, the road, music, moving forward. He had worked hard for that car. He started working at fifteen. He was the youngest man on the site. He drove a front-end loader and he could make it spin. He was fast, accurate, didn't waste a minute between loads. He appreciated how his father's mind worked, could anticipate his father as his father could anticipate him. They were both men of few words. They understood how to move through space. How things fit. They were agile.

But then suddenly he could not work anymore. Suddenly there were seven of himself commenting on everything in his brain. He felt tired. He couldn't speak. Didn't want to be up on the loader back and forth all day moving gravel, bumping around, hot, sweaty, thirsty, drained by the day's end. So quickly he became an embarrassment to his father.

He lost his car and a front tooth in a poker game. They picked him up by his jeans and threw him off the second-floor railing. He broke a rib, but he got up and spit at them. He spit blood at them, but he was the pathetic one, standing in the dirt in his blue cords and paisley shirt without so much as a cigarette or a dollar to buy one.

He hears what sounds like a ring. But then it holds in the air and he realizes it's a note, not a ring. It is clear and long. It isn't a voice. It isn't animal. Not owl, nor fox, nor teacup clattering with arms, nor flying fish, nor furry steak knives zinging in the wall behind his head. The feeling in him is deep and silent but reverberating. As if a bomb went off and no one heard it but him. But it's not violent, this bomb, it's a kind of singing.

He goes to the door and without pause he opens it, thinking he will hear the phone in the lobby downstairs and that it will be ringing for him. He leans his body out into the hall, but no, there is no ringing. He hears it still, but it's not outside the room. In fact, it is not even outside him. He closes the door quickly, his heart racing, but then suddenly he calms, as if the voices themselves are a kind of Gravol. They're not sharp, not piercing, or angry; they are soft. They make him feel as if he has five pairs of arms wrapped around him. As if his lungs might burst. If he opens his mouth it will be outside him, all around him, and these notes will take him up into the sky. He lets them vibrate in his chest. He lets the notes gather, but he doesn't want to let go. He can feel them wanting to squeeze out, pushing at his seams, but he holds them in until he is shaking with something that feels not at all unpleasant, even if it is deeply sad.

When her mother rises finally, from her sorrow, she begins to move forward, renewing her driver's licence, filling out forms, selling their house. They do these things, but now Annie has seen beneath, and behind, the actions. She strains against the emptiness there. After Joe's death it occurs to her that they are all pretending to be alive.

They move to Vancouver. They are pretending to be on holidays; pretending not to be running from grief, from the house overlooking the graveyard on Jubilee, the house that had become, for them, death; the house her brother inhabits still, if only in her mind, floating like a lotus flower, bumping into walls.

They go to Stanley Park. Look at totem poles and walk through the zoo. Line up for a photo on her aunt's patio in their holiday clothing: Therese in a yellow vinyl skirt, she in a blue flowered dress, Guddy in a brown kilt with a rust sweater, pompoms dangling around her neck; boys in grey slacks and striped T-shirts, their hair already a little too long for their father's liking. But they are on the west coast now, where things grow out of control. Behind them, hovering over them, you can see Joe's invisible hand pressing on Bjarne's shoulder.

That summer they picked raspberries. This is what she remembers: a small cabin in a field, surrounded by other cabins. Washing the children, putting them to bed. There is no toilet in the cabin, only bunks and a counter with a portable stovetop and small camping fridge: you can follow your nose to the outhouse. They are the only family. The other workers are young, transient.

They are a family that once owned a house. They are a family that once stood at the kitchen table while their father inspected their newly washed hands. Or perhaps that was just once? Didn't he appear in a crisp *white shirt, his hair freshly washed, face shaved, smelling of soap.*

It is summer and they are hot. She is suddenly unable to see. She trips over small rocks and bumps into doors. Now her childhood is blurry. They will pick raspberries, all of them, to pay for her glasses. They can see the bottom. They have nothing. They are in British Columbia now; they are away from Manitoba and its unbearable winter, away from the weight of loss.

Her father is elated. He will start work at the week's end. He will go away, of course, but he will send money, this is where the action is, this is where the great luck of resources is prime.

They will all pitch in. But her mother, suddenly asthmatic, surrounded by hops, by tall twisting vines, is unable to breathe. She lies on the back seat of the Valiant, doors wide open, while Therese runs back and forth with water and warm raspberries, the hops like power lines, and mountains, the coastal mountains gathering like so many hungry men, eager and ready to work.

They do not tell their aunts how they are spending their summer. Rule number 1: what happens in the family stays in the family. When they arrive on Sunday it is with a bucket of KFC. They are cleaned and scrubbed as if they lived in a real house. You didn't have to, her aunt says, wiping the counter in her kitchen, the doors to the backyard and swimming pool open, the sound of childhood running in and out of the water, the sounds of the suburbs, and leisure, and life far away from death.

Childhood has been inverted. She watches it crystallize, and can't imagine anything ever again being either sweet, or smooth.

ANNIE

Down the hill past the gravel pit, Annie slides her old Mustang to the right, to the motherlode, the blind spot. She navigates the trailer-park road, avoiding potholes on the one hand and crude speed bumps on the other, brazen feral cats lounging in the middle of the concrete and snot-nosed brats whacking each other with plastic bats. She pulls into the parking space of her mother's unremarkable blue 1980s trailer too abruptly, startling her cat, Missy.

Annie likes to keep moving, especially when the sun peeks out, as it's doing now, because it could last all of twenty minutes. She has been trapped all morning in her own trailer, waiting for her sister Guddy to call with news. She had phoned earlier from Seattle saying she was en route to Vancouver to see Therese and it wasn't good. That's all she said. She would call when she had more news. So Annie had spent the morning cleaning her own house, hovering by the phone but not being able to pick it up since the caller was, on the fifteen-minute mark, it seemed, her mother, and not her sister, and she did not want to speak to her mother.

Her mother's trailer – which Adel detests and inhabits under protest – is well-maintained, thanks to Annie, if homely. The trailer park is not a nice one, but her mother's trailer is framed by Thornhill mountain and so always has an air of drama about it. The baby-blue front is boxy, without the usual bay window, and the joey shack in need of repair. A light hangs down, smacking your head when you enter; the linoleum curls like tulip leaves at the edges. An old headboard holds her gardening equipment, tobacco tins of coins and screws and empty pill bottles. Cats have dug holes under the skirting and are likely breeding under the trailer like rats. No wonder Missy is always perched at the window on high alert.

The summer before, Annie put a garden in the front for Adel, but it had roses, not sweet peas, which didn't please

Adel, as was evident the one time she made her way to the front window to peer out. She never bothered to go outside, naturally; rather, she stood with the drapes pulled aside, her enormous glasses taking up half of her now shrunken, pale head. The look was disapproving, if comical. Her mother had brilliant timing, and when she wagged her finger and flipped Annie the bird in her see-through negligee, Annie could appreciate the humour.

The negligee, sent from Guddy, is a constant problem. 'Oh, Annie, I think the cable man has seen an old woman in a housedress,' Adel said, the poor young man desperately trying to avert his eyes. And afterward, 'Annie, you need to show a little more thigh, a little more cleavage: no wonder you have such trouble with men.'

As usual, the blinds are all closed. The cat perches on the railing, half ready to leap on Annie, who loves cats, but not this one. She's too intense. She stares with the power of ten cats. Like Adel, she's too intelligent and wily for her own good and she sticks out both in her looks and behaviour, prancing about the trailer court as if she were in Monaco at the arm of a prince. And her mother is insanely doting: Missy opened the door last night, she'll say, Missy turned the TV off and then on, Missy laughed at Leno. She sheds too much, destroys the furniture and will not sit still long enough for Annie to brush her. Adel thinks that the cat can speak to her too, and if Annie stays too long she has to listen to a conversation that goes something like *Missy, come Mama, or Missy, tell Mama*, with a long series of variations on the word *mawr* in response.

The cat really is strangely human, and responds directly when spoken to. She also acts like a guard dog, it's true. She can fetch cigarettes or tissues. *Too bad she can't bring me the clicker when I drop it*, the clicker being the enormous remote, or *Too bad she can't drag you home a husband.* Then, *Really, Annie, my cat has a better sense of humour than you do.*

Annie lets herself in and a waft of cigarette smoke mingled with the smell of Charlie hits her.

'Annie?'

'Yes, Mom, it's me.' The oddest thing about the cat is that for the past thirty-odd years Adel has professed to be allergic, dropping the cats she and her siblings saved from their dirty streets off in rich suburbs late at night while they slept. *I don't know, she whined to go out, and I let her,* she would say, or *I just think the cat wanted to live somewhere else.*

Annie isn't going to complain too much though, because the cat is like the child who doesn't want to leave, the one her mother always dreamed of. Like Guddy, the loyal baby who thought everything she did was hilarious, the mysterious, patient one always at hand to be petted, and as much as they all felt they owed a debt to the young Guddy, they now owe a greater one to Missy.

'Annie? I've been calling you all morning, why haven't you answered?'

'We spoke this morning,' Annie yells, 'and if you called, why not leave a message? I keep telling you to leave a message.' She kicks off her shoes and then, noticing the floor covered in cat hair and coffee grounds, puts them on again. Disgusting.

'We did not speak this morning,' her mother yells, 'and I don't want to talk to your machine.' Usually Adel is sleeping and Annie tries to sneak in and out, leaving a note on the counter about the food in the fridge, or the prescriptions she has picked up. Yes, her mother was once entertaining, but now she is simply irritating. There is always a squabble about something: number of pills, generic or not, change, or charges if Annie uses her card. All their lives, the simple task of going to the store for a package of Rothmans or a carton of milk was a source of enormous stress. *I gave you a twenty, where's my change*, and there was no adequate documentation. Even when the bill was seven and she could produce thirteen, there was something off. In the face of facts she could simply ignore all evidence that didn't suit.

'Haven't you heard me yelling? I could be dead in here.'

'I wish,' Annie says, opening the fridge to see whether or not the old woman has touched the chicken dinner from last night. She hasn't. Then, looking up, knocking the counter and throwing a bit of salt over her shoulder, she says, 'I didn't mean that. You know I didn't mean that,' and crosses herself, hoping it's left, right, up, down; she has long since forgotten the drill.

The woman next door cooked for Adel through the winter, but that ended abruptly. Annie assumes she got tired of the complaints, one after the other, for the three dollars she was paid for meals. *Is it a crime to want a little cauliflower or broccoli? Am I difficult in asking for mashed potatoes? I'm an old woman, Annie, I have false teeth: I can't be gnawing on a bit of raw carrot.*

Ludmilla wasn't doing it for the money, she told Annie, she was doing it because she found Adel charming, and at least initially had enjoyed listening to her stories. But she had taken up bridge, she said, and she no longer wanted to be tied to cooking regular meals. 'Your mother has had a life,' she said, shaking her head, 'there's no doubt about that.'

'Yes, well, don't believe everything you hear.'

Still, Ludmilla kept Adel's grass trimmed as neatly as hers, and took out Adel's garbage on the days Annie didn't make it by.

'Can't you come now? I'm having a heart attack in here. I'm terrified on my own. I need to go to the hospital!'

'You're not having a heart attack.' Annie takes a deep breath and makes her way down the narrow hallway, the cigarette smoke getting thicker with every step. She is also a smoker, but has, for years, relegated her habit to the outdoors. She gets to the door and clings to the wall, poking her head in.

'I am too,' Adel says, holding out a shaking, dry, flaky hand. 'I haven't slept all night,' she gasps. 'I had to use my oxygen, and then I couldn't get up to eat. I felt light-headed.' She coughs, snatching a Kleenex so she can catch the bit of lung coming up. Gobs of her go into the wastebasket by her bed, which overflows if Annie doesn't come by once a day to empty it. She could take all the excess fluid and clone an army of Adels, even if, as her father used to say, they broke the mould: *After your mother was born, God was terrified of women.*

Annie stands, trying not to look in if she can help it. Her mother is aging by the moment. Her eyes sunken under black circles. She no longer has an ounce of fat on her. And her skin becomes more translucent by the minute. She looks strained, slumped up against the wall, a glass of water and cup of cold coffee, several half-eaten candy bars on the night table by her bed, blankets askew in the overheated room, her once gorgeously troublesome legs now wrinkled and alarmingly thin, kicking out with the stubborn and sudden movements of a twelve-year-old. *Vivacious* was a word often used to describe her mother.

'You have emphysema, Mother, that's not new.'

'I know, I know, but this is different.' She holds out the hand again. 'Now my heart hurts too.'

She looks in pain, but then she always looks in pain. There is pain, or euphoria, not a lot in between. 'No, it's not different, Mother.'

'It is. I felt sweaty and my heart raced.' She lights another cigarette though one is already burning in the ashtray. 'Did Therese call you?'

'Why do you ask that? You know she never calls me.'

She hits her head with her fist the way she does when Annie doesn't read her mind. 'Because there is something wrong, that's why.'

'There is nothing wrong, Mother. Are you hungry? You didn't eat.'

'No, I am not hungry. I haven't slept. I am beside myself with worry. She won't call and I know. I just know.'

'What do you know?'

'That something is wrong.'

'Well, she is sick, Mother, she has been sick for years.'

'No, Annie, this is different. This is very different. There is something very, very wrong.'

'Why do you think something is wrong all of a sudden?'

Her mother rolls her eyes as if Annie is an idiot, gritting her teeth in frustration. 'Because the photograph of her, the one you hung over my dresser of her in the yellow vest, fell in the middle of the night.'

Indeed there are glass shards all over the dresser; her sister's photograph lies on the bed. Annie reaches for the photo. 'Are you okay?'

'Of course I'm okay, but I'm shaking, I feel dizzy. I think I'm having a heart attack. I took my pill, but I don't know if it was the right one.'

'Was it in the plastic container? The one Therese bought for you?'

'I don't use that stupid container.'

It is an old photo of Therese, from when she first came out and wore her hair short like a boy, and jeans and vests with no shirt under them. She is leaning against a wall in a yellow room, her thumbs in her belt loops as if to say, Yup, I'm a big old lesbian, deal with it.

'Well how do you know you've taken it if you're not using the daily container?'

'I took that pill. I mean the other kind, the one that Dr. Young told me to take when I'm having an anxiety attack.'

'An Ativan. Did you take an Ativan?'

'I can't find one. I thought you might have one.'

'Well, I don't. And if you've run out it's because you are eating them like candy again.'

'I am not. I think your brother steals them.'

Of course he steals them, Annie thinks, that's why he comes. 'Anyhow, you're not having a heart attack, so as long as you didn't cut yourself, I don't think there's a problem.'

'So now you're a doctor?'

'You just said you wanted an Ativan. It doesn't take a doctor to know how you get when you're anxious, Mom. It's more likely that you've had too much coffee.'

'There is no such thing as too much goddamn coffee.'

'Why are you shaking then?'

'Because something is wrong, dammit. And don't blame it on the coffee. I have my coffee, my TV and my cigarettes. That is all I have. You can't take what little I have.'

'No one is taking anything from you, Mother.'

'And my cat. I have my cat.'

'No one is taking your cat.'

'If you try putting me in a home you are taking my cat.'

'We are not putting you anywhere. Look, the photograph fell. I'm sorry if I didn't secure it properly, I told you I should wait and do it properly. Get an anchor and a picture hook, not just a nail.'

'You know damn well when a photograph falls it means there is something wrong, regardless of how it is or isn't nailed in, and besides, it is a proper picture hook. I know how to hang a picture.'

'What it means is you need to put an anchor in the wall so that the nail doesn't come loose, or a fly thing, something that splits on the other side of the panel to hold it in place. It doesn't mean anything other than that, Mom. You know I don't like this superstitious talk.'

'It's not superstitious. A black cat is superstitious. A one-legged man is superstitious. This is different. I told you about when my grandmother died.'

'Yes, you did, and your sister-in-law Juliet, I know. Now, give me the list, I have to go, Mom, I have a lot of things to do today. It's my day off, I'm back at work tomorrow for six days straight.'

'You always have to go.'

'I have a lot to do – '

'You have a lot to do – you always have a lot to do between your grandchildren and your job. You're so very important.'

'All right, that's it.' Annie grabs for the list, but Adel is quicker, and it disappears under the blanket. She sticks out her tongue. 'Want to dig for it?'

'God, Mother, you're disgusting.'

'Oh, where's your sense of humour? You lost that when you got so important? Oh wait, I forgot, you never had a sense of humour.'

What she would normally say is, *That tone is not nice, Mother*, but she has finally realized that it does no good whatsoever, so, she chooses to ignore.

'Have you heard from Ken?'

Annie goes for the glass, preferring, as always, to keep moving and avoid responding directly.

'Why can't you just sit for a minute? I'll do that later. I put the box there for the glass – '

'You won't do it later, Mom.'

'I will. Once I've calmed down. I'm still shaking.'

'I know you're shaking, Mom, and you have two cigarettes going.'

'I know I do. I'll have three if I want. It's my money.'

'Yes, I know, Mother, and if you burn down in your own bed?'

136

'I am not burning down, Annie.'

'How many sheets have you gone through in the past six months? And how many burn marks on your side table?'

'Can't you just talk to me like a normal person? Can't you make light conversation? Tell me about your daughters and your granddaughters until I relax. Or Ken, tell me about him. Did he call? Did you see him in town again?' Adel grabs Annie's arm, but Annie carries on picking the pieces up off her mother's dresser. 'I won't cut myself, Annie, just leave it!'

'You will, and you won't survive an afternoon in Emergency.'

'Has he not called? Is that the problem? Are you feeling neglected?'

'Let go,' Annie says, setting the empty chocolate box parallel to the dresser.

'Now you're going to scratch my dresser. I know you only have fake wood in your trailer, but here we have real wood. That is maple and you're going to scratch it!'

'I won't scratch anything if you let go.' Using her mother's cigarette pack, she slides the bits of broken glass into the box.

'I said *don't*, now that's final, Annie. For chrissake.' But Annie is out the door and down the hall, her own heart racing, and if she were at home and it wasn't the middle of the day she would take that Ativan she has in her purse.

'Oh, never mind,' Adel snaps, 'always running off to shop. Walmart this, Walmart that. You don't care for me, you just want my money.'

Ha, Annie thinks, but it doesn't matter what she says, Adel is already on to the next thought. She'll stub a cigarette out and immediately light another; all night like that, sometimes three or four packs a day, half of them burning like incense in the ashtray.

'When my grandmother died I wouldn't answer the phone,' she is yelling now. 'As soon as it rang, the room went cold. Like an icebox. She was the only one – '

'Who understood you, Mom, yes I know, she was the only one who understood you.' Annie puts the box in the garbage bag, thinking that she should empty it, yes, and then deciding no, she will wait until the end … not that there will be an end. No beginning, no end, just around and around.

'You don't know. You don't know anything. Why are you so impatient with me?'

'There was another derailment,' Annie says, opting for the change-of-direction approach. 'Seven cars went off. I heard it on the radio on the way over here.'

'Where this time?'

'Up the Nass. I was talking to Ken last week,' she says, filling her mother's dirty sink with water, 'and he said that the last time over in Kitselas, I think, a few cars went so far down the side of the mountain they had to get special equipment in to drag them up, and by the time they got to them they found black bears inside. They were stuck: they slid through the doors fine, but after a few days of gorging on fermented wheat they were fat and drunk and stuck inside. They had to shoot them.'

'I don't believe that.'

'Well, he said it. I don't know.' She is quick with the washing, rinsing too fast for her mother's tastes, but good enough for hers, and happy to have something concrete to do. 'He said they want to put a pipeline in along the river, but if they can't even maintain a rail line that doesn't constantly break down and cause so much trouble, how the hell do they think they're going to put in a pipeline to pump Alberta oil to the coast? And how do they think that will benefit us here? A few months of building and it will just be a leaky pipeline for us to deal with … '

'There was a bear in the trailer park last week. Just down the way. Attacked a dog.'

'They're hungry,' Annie yells back. 'Ken says they had to relocate a record number last year and they are expecting

138

more this year. More sightings than ever before on Ferry Island too.' These past few years, bears have been so hungry they walk into people's kitchens. One woman had her freezer turned over and all the bags of frozen salmon shredded. It isn't a coincidence that Annie had not bothered to make jam last year; the berries were so small they never did ripen.

'So you're seeing Ken?'

'I didn't say that, Mother.'

'Well, you'll have to cut your hair. You look like one of those soccer moms and no one wants to date a soccer mom. You might end up there, but you don't want to start there, if you know what I mean. I've said a million times, a man needs to imagine. You need to start wearing dresses again, Annie.'

'Is that right?' Annie imagines getting dressed to go to the group home and bathe her clients. Sure. That would be smart.

'Yes. Why don't you try on that red dress, the one with the polka dots. You could use those black heels. I know we have the same size foot, and you have my legs. You're a beautiful girl, Annie, you could turn heads.'

'Is that right?' Adel's femininity is more bullfighter than housewife. In fact, Annie can't remember a time when her mother was not in a dress and heels, even out in her garden, poised, hose in one hand, cigarette in the other, tits at hard angles in her cross-your-heart bra, one knee bent slightly in, and a smile that caused accidents. She was always flirting, always winking and encouraging. Annie looks at her reflection in the window and finds it hard to believe a haircut will help turn heads. Not that it might not have been true once, but she was too stupid to take advantage of it at the time. She married too quickly, to escape Adel, she likes to say, but she really did want to be a wife and a mother. That was what she wanted of life. Therese thought it was a deficiency, a limitation. Who in their right mind wanted to be a housewife?

She did. She likes being a mother. She likes cooking. She takes – or at least – took pride in her domestic skills, and why not? She's good at it. What she isn't good at is staying married, apparently. On the market again. At her age? She isn't interested. And even if she was, she can't figure out how to work with this aging thing. Yes, she has the bone structure, and she can appreciate the softness of her eyes, but the lines? The greying hair? She is too young to let it go white as her mother finally had after fifty years of dying it strawberry blond. But she doesn't like to fuss either. You just changed. One day your face required a whole other look, a whole other wardrobe to match it. How can she keep up?

'What are you doing in there? Will you bring me a fresh coffee when you come back?'

'Yes, I will, but I have to go now, Mom.'

'Just bring me the coffee first, or here, come and warm this one up. And try on the dress, will you? Why do you always have to run?'

'Because, as I've said, I have things to do.' She was more interested in dressing up when she was young. She is tired of the effort of being a woman. Annie is very tired of it. And since being a woman is what she's good at, what can she do now?

Annie wipes the counter hastily and hangs the J Cloth over the faucet to air out before heading back to the bedroom for the list. She needs the list to get the shopping done. That is apparently what she lives for, the shopping.

'And, Annie, don't you dare throw that glass in my trash.'

Right, Annie says to herself, turning around in the hall-way. She'll take it home. She can't put it in Adel's trash because once a week, usually an hour before the garbage is due to be picked up, Adel loses some bit of paper, or a piece of jewellery, or a pen, and they have to go through all the trash, sifting through bits of things wrapped tightly in

Kleenex, lists torn so tiny they look like confetti. It's never anything important. They rarely find it. Still, she is convinced, and they must see the thing through. Adel is also convinced there are secret bank accounts, and that her bank is ripping her off, and she is being overcharged for her cable, and her phone, and her lights. Annie takes the box of glass out and puts it by the door. 'When did you make this coffee?'

Nothing. Now she'll be pouting, Annie supposes, and fills a new cup, adding the appropriate sugar and milk and popping it in the microwave. There was a time when her mother wouldn't have had a speck of dirt in her house. Of course she had an army of brats to help her. When Annie and Joe were little she would have them down on their hands and knees washing the floor until she could wring the rag out so clear they could drink the water. Now the counter and the doors under the sink are covered with coffee stains and Annie doesn't even want to think of the bathroom …

'I saw a disturbing *Oprah* show,' her mother had confided recently 'Oh yes?' 'Yes, they had these women on who had an illness and I think I have it too.' 'You do?' 'Yes, they count things, and wash, over and over again.'

'Sounds familiar.'

'Yes, I am an excessive compulsive, and it is a registered illness.'

Get the note, get out, Annie reminds herself, but when she is back with the coffee Adel has the dress out, and the heels, and a low-cut blue satin dress with some kind of awful eighties hip brooch.

'Did I ever tell you what happened when my father died?' Adel is sitting upright on the bed, cigarette in hand. She nods toward the dress with a look that says, *Try it on.*

Annie yanks the window open as wide as it can go. 'I know the story, the cold, how you screamed, and how Dad picked up the phone anyway.' What else could have happened? The phone rings, you pick it up.

'But I asked him not to.'

The phone rings, you pick it up. She doesn't bother saying that out loud, having said it already a hundred times. What is the point? If her father had *not* picked up the phone, would the outcome be any different? Forty years the story lives on and why? There is no point to it.

'He picked it up anyway!' Adel says. 'Now try on the polka dots.'

'I'm not trying that on, Mom.'

'And I knew my father was dead. I knew it,' she says dramatically, hand across her forehead. 'I had an image of him hanging and I said, Don't pick it up, I don't want to know. And he did. Then I said, Don't tell me, I don't want to know, and he did.'

'I know you did, Mom, and I know he did.' And that, Annie supposes, is the point: that she is right. She knows everything, even before it happens. 'Can I have the list?'

'In a minute,' she says, calmly lighting another cigarette. Even in her ratty nightgown, not having bathed in weeks, her hair standing on end, there is an elegance about her mother that Annie both admires and detests. She has a drawer full of new nightgowns but likes to save them 'for later,' she says. She is happiest when holding court, and it doesn't matter that the court has become her bedside. The deeper into a story, the happier she is, and all she requires to be at peace is someone to listen to her. Annie can see she is trying to launch in, to get comfortable in a story, and Annie debates letting her start. She is surprisingly calm after spending this much time in the trailer, still, she has to manage exposure; it's like radiation: low levels she can manage, but you can't see the effects until much later, when your hair starts to fall out and your internal organs shut down.

The day she heard her mother was moving back to Terrace, Annie went to her doctor thinking she was having a heart attack. Her doctor prescribed Ativan. Adel had burned all of her bridges in Surrey; her sister, her sister-in-law, her nieces and nephews, no one visited – even Jerry had turned his back on her, and with her health failing, she had no choice but to move north to be near Annie, and Annie had no choice but to welcome her.

Therese warned Annie that she was suffering dementia. She had tried to get her diagnosed when Adel ended up in the hospital in Langley, which had nearly killed them both. Adel's doctor told Therese he wouldn't put anything on record where her mother was concerned. Therese reported him to the medical board, which made him even less willing to discuss anything. Over the phone he told Annie, 'Histrionic, perhaps, but there's no medication for that.'

But at that hospital someone prescribed the same pill her brother had been on before he started the shots, and someone else told Therese that Adel was manic-depressive, but no one would write it down, and after a while Annie wasn't sure who to believe and so believed no one. What they can be certain of is no dementia and no early-onset Alzheimer's. But that's about it.

Therese was right though, she forgets things. Not the past, no, not the past, that is as bright as ever. It's the present that gives her difficulty.

'I knew when your father's father died too,' she says. 'I didn't want to leave him. I loved him so much even though we didn't understand a word each other said. He was so gentle, so understated. I was sitting on the sofa and suddenly it was cold. Like I was in a freezer. Then I saw your grandfather turn and wave.'

'And are you cold now, Mom?'

She pauses. Cocks her head. 'Why are you asking that?'

Annie enjoys the momentary squirm. Death has held court in their family her entire life. This going over and over all of the deaths except the one death that really solidified her mother's grief. All their grief. The only death she never, ever brought up. No one did. The death that had been erased, and enshrined, that had, in a sense, frozen them all in time. Had she known about that before? Had she seen it coming? Is that why she fought with Jean that night, and the many nights after? The constant bickering? The cruelty? Annie is tempted to toy with her, or worse, to ask her outright, but it makes her feel, well, like her mother – cruel – so she lets go. 'Because the window is open. Are you cold now?'

Adel pauses, assesses, and then settles back onto her pillow. Tentatively. 'The cat is out,' she says, cautiously. 'That's why the window is open, and no, I am not cold.' She stares at Annie, skeptical but clearly relieved to be on the other side of whatever might have opened up between them.

Annie has to hand it to her though: she's right; there is a hole opening in their world today. And, as usual, they are talking around it. She doesn't want to think of it, can't quite think of it, and certainly won't tell her about it. Not just yet. No, she won't say anything, having given Guddy her word.

Annie feels calm for a moment; for so long she has operated under the assumption that she can keep nothing from her mother, and now it seems she can. Just for a moment perhaps, but she can withhold something.

Adel has convinced them all she is psychic, that there is no outside of her, of family. And yes, she is powerful, formidable, even now, so much thinner and frail, weathered and spindly, but she can rise up. Annie has seen her take a grown man down with one punch, smack a police officer in public for being racist, and without hesitation take her and Therese by their hair and bang their heads together on more than one occasion. She seems able to tap into some extra strength when she shifts into her rage mode.

That power has a cost, Annie realizes now; in a way, she has to turn herself inside out to get at that rage. Or maybe outside in? In any case, now the instances are less frequent. Less intense. And Annie can also see how she suffers for them. Days of sleep, of depression, follow any outburst. And that is perhaps why her mother has become agoraphobic. She no longer drives, no longer owns a car. Unimaginable to Annie, for her mother always seemed to be as one with her various cars.

'There was a bird in here too,' her mother says, calmly chewing on a caramel and smoking, her free hand twisting the wrapper into a knot.

'I told you to put a bell on that cat.'

'It wasn't the cat.'

'No,' Annie says, watching her mother take one wrapper and twist it to another wrapper, 'I suppose not.' She will find a chain of wrappers when she cleans next. She will also find a notebook filled with names, starting with A and moving through to Z, hundreds of names, alphabetized. On one side women's names, the other side men's names, meticulously written in her mother's formal cursive handwriting, favouring the names of movie stars and the 1940s, her mother's decade of choice. She had taken it to her doctor once as proof of her insanity and he had laughed at it, and her. 'Obsessive yes, but insane?'

'I'm old, Annie, I haven't lost my mind.'

'No, you haven't.'

'No, and nor have you lost that weight you keep talking about losing.'

Nor have you lost your tongue, or your ability to wriggle situations around, Annie thinks, but she keeps that to herself.

'It's responsible to put a bell on the cat,' she says.

'I said it wasn't the cat!'

'So you say.'

'A bird flew in.'

'I heard.'

'You didn't hear, you don't listen, you never do. Maybe you need your ears cleaned out? Then you would hear when opportunity knocked. You would be out and about, listening, and when you found something you wanted you would grab it by the goddamn balls and hold on to it for dear life. You would have a spine. A little get up and go. You wouldn't be cowering here in grey track pants waiting for a call from a goddamn lumberjack.'

And there it was. The turn.

Annie stands having a cigarette on the front steps next to Missy who stares out with her wide, astonished eyes. She should leave. She should let Adel and her trailer fall into complete disrepair. The social worker told her as much. No one can help until she hits bottom. They said that about Bjarne too, though, and it isn't right. Why wait until a person is ravaged by life? Why wait until there is no return? It seems to Annie that all of her life she, and her family, have been dangling. Not hitting bottom, but never stabilizing, and certainly not moving up.

On the other hand, her daughters are okay. They have gone on to have healthy families, good jobs. She has three grandchildren whom she sees regularly. Her daughters are smart enough to keep their distance from Adel and think she should too, but then who will care for her? There isn't anyone else. Jerry is in Vancouver, and anyhow, completely severed ties long ago. Guddy in New York. Bjarne does what he does. So, back again. The circle. The thing that really pisses

Annie off is that Adel still operates under the assumption that she is helping Annie.

The heat shudders to a stop. The entire trailer seems to settle back onto the earth and, along with it, Annie's heart rate. She goes back in, determined somehow to get the list and carry on. If she doesn't, it will start all over again tomorrow and she has no time tomorrow. This way she might buy herself a break, and she might need a break.

She stops outside Bjarne's door, where she notices a large brown stain, not a coffee stain, something nastier, and this really, really pisses her off. He's a slob. Yes, he's sick, but he can get up and empty his ashtray, and he can pick up after himself. But he won't. She has seen him drop a half-eaten sandwich on the floor and step over it. He doesn't have to live this way. She could set him up with a house cleaner, have someone do his shopping, but like Adel, he is stubborn. He has little left in his life and he isn't about to have her arrange it, so he lets things around him go until he is nearly cocooned in his own filth.

'You better tell Bjarne to wash his own sheets,' she yells, trying to sound forceful.

'He does.' Adel, now with the indignant little-girl voice: 'He's such a good boy, Annie.'

'He's a man, Mother, a middle-aged man, and he should be able to clean up after himself – '

'He's so good to me. He's so gentle. I don't know what I would do without him – '

'You better tell him I won't be coming around to clean up after him. And to clean whatever the hell this is on the carpet.'

'He loves you,' Adel says. 'And you never visit him.'

'I visit him. Not often anymore because he won't leave his room long enough to have a coffee with me in the Pizza Patio six steps from his room, or walk with me to the mall so I can buy him clean underwear. He doesn't want to tear himself away from *Judge Judy*, and I don't want to go and sit in his stinking room. And you know he's gotten weird with the Bible, muttering about goodness and righteousness.'

'That's not fair,' Adel says. 'He's sick. It isn't his fault. He sits here with me calmly. He keeps me company, and it's good he reads the Bible. There is nothing wrong with the Bible.'

'Really? Is that why you call after he leaves and complain about how spiteful he's been? How he has stolen your money? How he complains when you ask him to do anything? How he spills coffee all over your kitchen cupboards and floor and won't wipe it up?'

Adel twists her wrapper, not looking up at Annie, standing by her bed now. First her mother, then her baby sister, then four husbands, and two children and grandchildren, and then her work in the group home. She wants some peace in her life. Something without chores or guilt attached, thank you.

And then, the soft voice: 'Will you be picking up my cigarettes? I'm almost out.'

'You know when they come, Mother. You know exactly when they come, and you know that I can't get them before that.'

'Well, then can you pick up a tin of tobacco for me until they come so I can roll my own? Or just a carton from Safeway? And will you please call Therese and find out what's happening? I know there's something going on. I have been calling for days, on the hour, and she doesn't pick up. She doesn't even hang up on me. At least when she does that, I know she's alive.'

'She hasn't spoken to you in months, Mother. You told me last week you couldn't imagine talking to her again. You said that you had given up on her, and on Jerry too.'

'I know, but I haven't had a letter or a call. She always sends something for Valentine's Day. You know how she is, every holiday a card. Was there anything in the mail?'

'No, Mother, there was nothing but flyers,' Annie says, which is a lie since she hasn't checked the mail.

'Will you call her then?'

'I will call,' Annie relents.

'Will you call now? From here?'

'She'll know the number, Mom. She won't pick up. I don't even know if she'll pick up when I call.'

'What about Guddy? Has she talked to Guddy? Guddy hasn't called, and she usually calls at least every other day.'

'I'll call them both tonight. I promise. I'll call you if there's any news.'

'Call even if there isn't. And Jerry too. Don't tell him I asked you to, Annie, just call. He's your brother.'

'I'll be back with groceries anyway, Mom.'

'I can't be blamed, Annie, she was like a wild animal in my house. I was frightened for my life. Have you ever seen her like that?'

'Like what?'

'So angry.'

'Yes, I've seen angry.' I've seen a lot of angry, Annie thinks, and between Therese and Adel it's hard to say who could be more angry, or more terrifying.

'I thought she was going to kill me. She was like an animal, stalking me. Cold as a snake. Ready to strike. Everything I said to her she just laughed at, *Is that right, Adel, Oh, you think so, Adel*, with that smirk, like she had a demon in her. I wouldn't have called the police otherwise, Annie. I didn't know they would kick her out like that, without her medication.'

'I'm sure you didn't, Mom. I'm sure Therese understands.'

'I didn't know she would drive like a crazy woman, or crash on the freeway, or that she would have been without her medications for the weekend, or lose her car.'

'I know, Mom. No one is blaming you.'

'They didn't tell me. I didn't see them. I was locked in my room, afraid for my life. I don't know what I thought would happen, but she was so crazy.'

'I have to go now,' Annie says. 'I'll clean the bathroom when I come back with your groceries.'

'Annie, you know how much I appreciate all you do for me? You've been such a help. You have always been such a help.'

Annie would very much like to take her mother at her word. 'I know, Mom. Give me your list.'

Adel hands the list over. 'Don't forget my *Enquirer*s and some Polident. And at least bring me my flyers in the meantime. I want something to read. I need to distract myself. Oh, and Annie, buy yourself something nice from me for Valentine's Day.'

Annie spins her wheels on the gravel, nearly missing the road and sliding down the embankment just before the turnoff to Ferry Island. Fuck it, she thinks, and rolls slowly down the embankment to the parking lot. What if this is Therese's last day? What should she be doing? What was appropriate? She could effect no change in her life, let alone anyone else's, and she had no one to turn to. Well, maybe Guddy, but she hardly knew Guddy anymore, and she was off living in America and doing whatever. And Therese never wanted to spend time with her. To talk to her. She treated Annie like she was a child. She has always been indignant. Difficult. Proud. Stubborn.

And, of course, Therese's struggle is nearing the end. She feels tight in the chest. Her heart, as if there are things attached to it, tiny tentacles like the sea urchin she saw at the aquarium in Stanley Park years ago. The chenille texture of the sea floor under Barkley Sound, or was that Sechelt? Was it Therese who brought up the chenille, like the bedspreads they had when they were kids? Why is she thinking of this? Because it was Therese who managed her interactions with Vancouver? Who took her and the girls to the aquarium and pointed these things out? Who sent her photographs of herself and her girls at Third Beach to commemorate their visits?

Whatever. She loves her sister, but she doesn't understand her. Frankly, she is exhausted just thinking of her. She pulls on the parking brake and opens the door, but as soon as the fresh air hits her, she feels a surge of self-loathing. As if she is somehow undeserving of the clean air. She closes the door again. Starts the car. But she can't move. She turns it off. Starts it. Turns it off. She should go home so she is there for Guddy's call. She should go to Walmart and get her mother's groceries. She should go clean her mother's bathroom. Maybe should go to her daughter's for coffee. Beth would be home. No. She opens the door again and hits what feels like a glass wall between her and her next thought and movement. Maybe she is having a heart attack. Maybe she is the one who needs to be listened to. Maybe she is the one who needs to cry. She looks around; no one is there, no one is watching her. She could cry now, if she wanted. She closes her eyes and leans back against the car, but nothing comes.

Still, she feels light – despite the added pounds, which seem like air today. It is February, Valentine's Day, as her mother reminded her, and unusually warm. The island is thick with cottonwood, bare now, unlike most of the other trees in the region. She lifts her foot and gets a waft of that gorgeous river-earth-mixed-with-mulch smell, weeks too soon.

She tries to move again, but no, she hits her head on what feels like something very hard and clear. 'Sometimes remaining where you are is the most difficult thing,' Therese said once. 'Sometimes those are the heroes. The ones who stay.' Therese also has this theory that their mother sees things

151

most people don't see. And Bjarne too. 'Normal people call it insanity,' is what Annie said then. And she, Annie, of sound mind, refused insanity then and she refuses it now.

'No,' Therese said, 'not insanity. Sensitivity. Intuition. Lack of skin.'

Well, maybe Annie is also all of those things. She takes a deep breath and pushes herself through the wall, and soon enough she is walking in the empty campground to the outer trail.

She will smoke and walk; it's her way of staying healthy. It's a compromise. And why doesn't she call Guddy herself, she thinks. She's always calling from her cellphone, which means Annie can call her in return. Why has she not thought of that? Fine, she will have her walk and then she will get groceries, drop them off, go home, and call. And maybe she will fly down anyhow, and maybe when she gets home there will be some flowers on the table from Ken, or a chocolate heart from one of her daughters. Some slight gesture so she doesn't have to worry about being unloved now, on top of everything else.

She feels Therese for a moment, walking beside her. 'Why do you always need validation,' Therese says, 'particularly from men?' 'I don't need validation from anyone,' Annie says out loud, so confidently she almost believes herself.

She marches past the campgrounds, picnic tables at odd angles, pits of hardened ash and wet wood, here a bit of twine, there the bright blue of a Kokanee cap, the air, moist and thick, draping reassuringly around her neck. She is very aware of the wheezing of her chest, her feet snug in her shoes, her glasses pinching her nose, her cigarette smoke wafting around her, and feels, despite everything, quite powerful as she heads through the bush, letting every creature know that a human is coming through.

She watches her mother like other children might watch the sky. She is changeable; she must be studied with the meteorologist's meticulous eye: in mood – now approachable, now playful, now to steer clear of, now to soothe, now to feed, now to tend, now to remain calm – but also in shape – now dark and smouldering, now thin and listless, now like a tornado hard and black.

Her mother is a distant land, too wild, too unpredictable to visit. She can tell by their interactions. They stare across the miles, marvelling, but not curious enough to venture out. They see behaviours like dandelions that can, and must, be plucked out. But she has sat with her mother in the summer with butter knives digging down into the root systems of dandelions, her mother with her cigarette and glass of 7 Up, humming, her mother with her implausible presence, her sudden bursts of knowledge, and warmth. Her enormous, open and shattered heart: You have to get it all out, or you're wasting your effort.

Every childhood has its first memory. Hers is of her mother weeping. The room is black and white. She is on her back, her feet in the air. Her mother lies across the chenille bedspread shielding her eyes, from what she can't tell. They have taken Joe and Annie from her. Her father has conspired with the doctors who suggest that Adel won't survive the pregnancy, let alone take care of two babies, so they have sent them to relatives in France for a year. Adel put her hair in pincurls, buttoned her wool coat over her pregnant belly, and walked them to the plane, waving them off as if they were going to the park for the afternoon. After that she collapsed.

For over a year they were in France, almost a year after she was born. For a year there was only Therese and her mother. Therese drank in her mother's sorrow.

154

She sees the two of them reflected in the bedroom mirror. She can smell her mother, see her burying her tears, she can even roll over if she tries hard enough, she can roll over and be nearer.

All that year she watched her crepe-thin mother lie, unable to pull herself up off the bed. The world is at sea, the boat of domesticity always threatening to capsize; Adel daily washes the decks, hoists the white sheets in the air to dry. Upright. Therese wants to be upright. Later, when she starts school, she will come home at lunchtime and still her mother is lying like this, sobbing. She opens the curtains, windows, makes the coffee, sits by her side, soothing. Later, she will find her mother on the bathroom floor with an empty bottle of pills and she will pick up the phone. Later, she will find her mother too sad to move and she will dance by her bed.

The tears never really left. They calmed but carried on, and after Joe's death they came back with force. Her crying the rhythm of their childhood.

Alone in her bed, childhood dripping from the rafters around her, she finds solace in attempting to take account: this is the book of the generations of Adam ... And she would work backwards as far as she could. She thought of Joe as the sacrifice, Joe as the saviour of childhoods. She worked out equations in which she could imagine them all spared.

Sometimes she wakes from a dream in which her house is on fire and she is attempting to locate her siblings in the blaze. She flies above, and in, finds herself bumping her head on the ceiling, wakes in a sweat, barely clinging to mattress, and has to wait until her body settles back onto the bed. She rolls into a ball in the

155

middle of the bed. She rolls to the corner. She slides down the stairs to her mother's bed in the dining room, for which they have no use, eating as they do in the kitchen, and there she is assured of life, she is calmed by the light leaking out through the sliding door, her mother firmly at the head of the ship, steering them through the long, long night.

THERESE

The real.

As soon as she considers the word *real* she feels heavy, her hip, her kidneys, their new lace texture, weighing on her. Metastasized, her oncologist said: ribs, lungs, vertebrae and likely her bones. No organ that was not under attack. She elbows up so she can see the sky beyond the bit of scrub maple that strokes her drain spout all day. Of course she hears it; she hears everything, even the inside of her body eating away at itself. Is that real enough?

She has never understood what people think realism is: how is it possible to be modern, to be queer, to be liberal, and to still see the world as any kind of representation other than structures, signs, textures, gestures, strokes, impermanent, transitory? People confuse style with reality, opinion with fact. Aren't we all seeing something unique? Seeing from the perspective of our experience, our bodies, of our particular threshold for pain or pleasure, our histories, our discomfort, or capacity for colour and shape and articulations?

She is painfully aware that she is body now more than ever. She is also aware that people like Helen, who, despite Therese's bad behaviour, has not given up on her, would say that this isn't true, even though much – her moods, her opinions – is chemical, biological, mercurial. Just the opposite is true, in fact. She lifts her comforter, rearranges herself, though the thought that perhaps she is just thinking she is doing this flickers. She hears Guillaume, her neighbour's son, taking out his bicycle. He is quiet. He knows she is sleeping, knows she hasn't come out onto the terrace, and if she were feeling up to it she would, and she would call down to him and he would tell her about his Pokémon cards, or his beans, which he planted in the window and which have not yet sprouted. His face is beautiful. Soft. Perfect. He is the only one who notices whether her blinds are open or closed, whether her doors are flung wide, who understands her sensitivity as a matter of course. A tug of wrist, a gaze, to assess her status and he adjusts himself accordingly.

He thinks: she isn't at the window today, but the light is on, she must therefore be inside, which means inside her mind, her head, is in need of quiet. He will hold the door until it clicks and walk his bicycle to the sidewalk, will not call out randomly until he is in the street. Small gestures, but huge really, coming from a nine-year-old boy. The tiny click of the lock is the only trace of him, his thin arms reaching out under his too-large T-shirt, so silent.

She assumed this attention to be the norm, but now she realizes, with some sadness, that such gestures are exceptions. There is very little she would like to hear more of these days. There is very little that surprises her anymore either. Having no expectations makes life easier. She is still annoyed by people's reactions, yes, but no longer flinches the way she once did, as if she were being whipped. She no longer experiences stupidity as a lashing. A personal affront. On the other hand, surrounded by idiots, what else can one think? She does give in sometimes, she does feel herself tense when she hears her other neighbour, a former crack addict now dying of AIDS who still carries on as if it were 1983, coming in with street life, partying into his demise. Even he, as irritating as he is, has more visitors than she does. And perhaps that is why, more than her body, it is her heart that feels ravaged. Her heart, the only healthy organ she possesses, is broken. Such sentiment. She never was one for sentiment, and yet it is her core now. I am broken-hearted, she says. My broken is hearted.

If that can be said to be real. It's technically true, but she mistrusts even that. The body certainly seems real at this moment, and the drugs that go into her daily seem real, and the noise from the neighbours, that too seems real, but in truth she thinks there is a body under all of this that is her real body. And perhaps more surprising than that is the fact that the past seems even more alive, looming all around her. After all these years of trying to distance herself from it, here it is, a perpetually incoming tide.

I was a girl. I did cartwheels on the lawn in summer, I ran behind the city truck with its spray of DDT, I had dreams of strange worlds with many-toed animals, and humans with seven hearts and six eyes who could breathe underwater. I saw the forest as a canopy, bark as a breathing fungus, the earth reaching up to caress my feet. I wanted to do good things, I imagined huge canvases, great swaths of colour, I wanted to create beauty; I wanted to do no harm.

She rearranges herself on the Pema Chödrön sheets Helen has bought for her, and which feel good under her sore body and bring back pleasant memories. Those days on Salt Spring Island with prayer flags stretched down to the bay, the arbutus peeling, nights listening to Aretha, doors open wide and small boats gathered in the bay; that New Year's Eve, the water so flat they all thought it looked like a skating rink, the lanterns they made sitting in the bay a bright audience for their rituals and, like Orlando, she felt like taking Helen's hand and skating across the ice. The sea froze right across the strait and they glided across waves of smooth ice; she knows natural ice would not be flat and skatable, but she can afford the luxury of editing out such details now.

She hasn't encountered ice since childhood and in truth doesn't miss it. She prefers warmth, prefers light, and prefers a lack of rain; guiltily this last one, for she knows it will be part of global warming. *Global warming* is not a helpful term, and her cheeks flush suddenly with anger at the way people treated AIDS because it was introduced as a gay epidemic. How language can undermine, how so much time and energy is wasted because of what we label something. Why had we not called it *climate change* rather than *global warming* right from the start? Now with every unseasonably warm day the idiots say, 'If this is global warming, bring it on … '

The sheets are made of hemp, and that knowledge makes her feel better too, wondering as she often does whether people will wake up to the possibilities of the planet anytime soon. The new order is disorder: decentralized, mindful entrepreneurialism, not toxic, not narrow-minded, not sweeping the hidden costs under the rug. And wrestling the word *family* back too: *family values* meaning valuing families of all kinds, even animal families (why not?). It means making ethical decisions, not putting one's children into a private school and letting others suffer. She wants to see that moment: the shifting of values. She believes it is coming and feels a rush of excitement at the prospect: fuel cells, wind energy, pedestrian cities: a combination of dispersing energy systems and condensing populations and carbon footprints. And she does what she can to realize it. She has no income, but she sends ten dollars a month to the Suzuki Foundation. She sends emails to the prime minister. She signs petitions for Kyoto. She carries shopping bags. She turns off the lights. Powers everything down. Of course it isn't enough, but one does what one can. One wants to take less from the world. One wants to leave it unscathed. One attempts to lead the life one admires. One wants to carry out her own garbage. To clean up her own shit and bury it alongside.

Her back aches, robs her of sleep. So many thoughts, confusion, pain. The pain gets her thinking of her father. *My* father, she thinks. *Mine.* She lays claim. She admits that now, what she always knew, her sense of having a special connection with him. She had the language, the engaged history, and the looks. A mirror image. She held a grudge, yes. Hated her siblings. Particularly Guddy for her silence, for not telling her he was so sick. (She never was trustworthy – always held back, and worse, knew better.) They never had a ceremony for Joe, and then they didn't have a proper one for their own father. How many chances does one family need to learn to acknowledge life? And death? To distinguish one moment from the next? And now, she supposes, hers is next. Well, they won't be acknowledging that; she won't let them.

The real is what we agree on, she thinks.

She takes a breath. If she had taken to books in the proper order, she sometimes thinks. If she'd had a more orderly education, she could make better sense, not have to come up with these thoughts on her own, a weaker version of what someone better read might have come up with more precisely ... but no, she has her own thoughts, and she bangs away at them, trying to build a functional dwelling out of mismatched pieces of wood.

There is no light today and no light means what? Means she is without energy. She is without hope. She will sink to the bottom. She will linger at the back of the cave. Her thoughts like boulders weighing her down. Let space enter your thoughts, she remembers Helen saying, and she does, she breathes and lets space enter and slowly, slowly ...

Staying positive seems to be the only thing left to strive for. After a lifelong aversion to the simplistic (and, she would argue, aggressive) thinking of the positivists, she now sees the benefit of it. The pain makes it more difficult. She wants to say it is *all pain*, these flashes of anger. But of course that isn't true. Even she knows that isn't true. All these years and she still has no clue where the rage comes from. It surges in her and she feels herself rise up, physically, wanting to engulf whatever the source of anxiety seems to be, which is probably not what she thinks it is ... She knows who she blames for the rage, but she can't say that she really *is* to blame for the rage.

The light in her room, or lack of it, reminds her of her summer living in the stairwells of the apartment buildings around Guildford. She hid her bedding, in a waterproof bag, deep in a hedge, carried a small bag with her personal items, begged for quarters outside Woodward's when she needed food, or to do laundry, shoplifted when she needed. Came and went at her leisure. Saw the sun coming up, or the moon tracking the mountains. At that time everything was open in apartment complexes; she just walked into the laundry rooms and swimming pools. She stole a bathing suit from a lost and found at the recreation centre and lounged with friends in backyards in Birdland. They went to parties in the bush around the mall, and near Johnston Heights, and although there is very little she has to say about that area that is good, in truth she remembers the summer fondly.

She didn't know it at the time, but she was in love with M. and soon found herself living with her family, babysitting and cleaning in exchange for room and board.

It wasn't the first time Therese had found refuge with friends. She ran away at twelve and lived with Donna and her family in Birdland, and she was thirteen when she moved in with Dave and Marilyn as a live-in nanny. So you see, she thinks, she tried to keep her distance ... and yet it's too compelling, family. Too much pull. Too complicated, her feelings for her mother, who makes her heart both skip and sink; too frustrating, the potential with Guddy, whom she worries about but couldn't quite save, though nor can it be said she has abandoned her entirely either.

Random thoughts now: horses in a field, a boxcar with many people sitting, staring out over the plains. I've been thinking of my future, Therese thinks, it has something to do with mud. Something to do with the way we make beauty out of sweat. Sweeping landscapes. Every moment a knife or a balm. It occurs to Therese that building these moments one by one is a way to tell a story. She can simply move toward the light, which is image. Narrative emerges from movement. Sequence. Little narratives, she thinks. Like snapshots taken with little thought. Standing in a street in Paris, staring after her cousin who left her for a Muslim man they had met in the street, a man she would eventually marry, a man who drove a wedge between Therese and her cousin. The way time expanded for her the first time she set foot in the Louvre. Or the way the bullets popped in the air like balloons the night she was caught in a police chase in Paris. The day rain fell like sheets in Montparnasse and they ran as if they were moving through laundry hanging from a line. The caves of Lascaux, how they took her breath away. She and M., that first summer of travel, sleeping in the Black Forest. Touching the walls outside Château de Chambord. (Or Chenonceau, she can't recall now, the same place they hid all the art from the Louvre, wasn't it? In any case, she felt the weight of bodies lined up againt the wall and shot, still falling at her feet.) Hitchhiking through France with her portable record player – a gift from Adel – and several of their favourite albums. They arrived in Paris the day of their graduation and danced the night away together in a bar on the Left Bank. Men cut in, they moved with them, but suddenly Therese saw M. in a new way ... and M. saw Therese. They stared past the vari ous men, into each other's eyes.

M. had an afro then, and her lips glistened. She wore tight pants that flared around her ankles and necklaces that plunged below her neckline; she plucked her eyebrows, stood tall, her neck like a giraffe's, seeing everything high above Therese's head. She made up Therese's face, tucked her hair behind her ears. It was long then and straight. M. knotted it around her wrists and said it was like silk.

She wants to think of M. To sink into details: her hair, her eyes. She wants to allow herself to think of M. because for so many years she did not. She had no idea women could make love, and M. had an orgasm so effortlessly, like bumping up against a chair – it was extraordinary, but she wouldn't, couldn't have one herself, can hardly stand to think of it even now. Now she knows it was simply priggishness, but at the time she thought that if she did she would somehow be marked or ruined, would not be able to have sex with a man. Now it's embarrassment; then it was ignorance. Then it was an inability to see another path beyond the fact that they would each marry, have children, move to the suburbs, even though neither of them was on that path, or wanted that path; though M. did end up married, it was childless, elegant, urban.

The first time they kissed was in her aunt Lolotte's stone apartment with the view of the old church in the Alps. Bells went off on the hour, and she kept thinking of her father leaping from the steeple in his homemade parachute. She was stiff with fear even in the quietest moments, but M. came and came in the cell-like bedroom where no doubt the only shudder before and since has been her virgin aunt creaking up and down from prayer.

They listened to Marvin Gaye, Stevie Wonder and Elton John. They were seventeen, in Europe, and had the rest of their lives before them. She kept a journal of this time, and the stairwell summer too. But words are too raw. She burned all that writing and later shredded all evidence of M. because it made her sick to read it. Not because the events upset her, but because there was no I in the narrative, or at least not a real I. The text was gloss, the text was external detail, the text revealed the depths to which she had not been present in her life, in her own narrative, and that made her ill.

She is currently taking OxyContin 80mg up from 20mg, Prednisone, Fluoxetine 20mg, Docusate and Oxycodone for breakthrough pain. If she is honest with herself, she knows the days have begun blurring one into the other with no distinction, nothing to mark the time, aside from the fluctuating effectiveness of her pharmaceutical cocktails. All her life she has avoided any drugs at all, trying in her way to have nothing to do with doctors or health care, an institution she is extremely suspicious of after seeing the many prescriptions her mother came out with, and none of them any use.

Now she sees how impossible it is to treat anything, to understand even the most basic ache, or sorrow. After a lifetime of attempting to filter, to justify, to order, she realizes this is impossible. How can living be boiled down to a periodic table? The whole solar system is out of balance; she feels as if she is spinning out of control, and the more she thinks the more she spins. She clings to the window ledge as if she is in a hurricane, sweat salting her bed.

Life is so much more precarious than anyone wants to accept. All around her, bodies shooting like stars through space. Joe, of course, and then Dave and Marilyn, a couple she babysat for when she was thirteen, whom she had watched fall off a balcony. One minute they were standing in the sun, in their formal outfits, ready to go for a celebration – a wedding anniversary? A promotion? She can't recall, only that she had come from the kitchen with a glass of Coke. They were leaning against the railing, laughing. They wanted her to take a picture of them. 'Catch us now,' Dave said, and Marilyn, twice his size, had leaned back, laughing. Then quite suddenly gravity took over and her feet were in the air, and then his, he having turned to grab her, and they were both gone, and there she stood with her glass of Coke.

Let me out, she is thinking, *someone come and unplug the house!* Is she screaming this or is she thinking it? Is her body spinning on the inside or the outside? Is the light inside of her or out?

She can no longer tell.

It reminds her of when she sunk into a snowbank and got stuck. She had snuck out of the house after dinner in her snowsuit and hiked up on the mounds surrounding the ice rink down the street. The banks were so high she could see over the roughly erected boards and watch the men playing hockey, the thwack of the puck, the swish of skates like music, and suddenly she sunk down, her arms at her side, and every time she struggled she went deeper, packed the snow more tightly around her. But she didn't panic, no, she kept very still, staring up at the lights from the skating rink illuminating the snow and ice, and she began to sing. She sang and sang until her mother's head appeared above her and within moments she was wrapped in a blanket, with a cup of warm milk.

Pema Chödrön isn't a colour, or a vegan recipe; she is a woman, a Buddhist teacher Helen reads and follows. She is like the first five minutes of the golden hour, facing west, under an arbutus, with a cocktail, a good friend and Nusrat Fateh Ali Khan playing, out of doors, in May or September, on a Tuesday for preference.

The world has calmed momentarily. She is thankful, not for God but for Gravol: every variety and flavour of it. With Gravol and stillness she can wade through the worst of the upheavals. And they are coming more frequently: the lows, the highs, but more lows and lower ones in a way. She is hungry, smells food, doesn't want to eat but enjoys the smell. Perhaps Susan has come. She took the dog out for a walk and was going to bring coffee. (She continues to bring the dog despite Therese's obvious discomfort, her dislike of doggie smells no matter how charming, and of course the dog is charming, a mini-Susan on a leash ...) She has been to the Drive and bought olives, and though she can't think of eating those now she is thankful for Susan and the olives and everything she brings and half-hopes it's chocolate. She is in a sweet phase and craves cheesecake, chocolate, licorice allsorts and Almond Roca, which between Helen and Susan, she gets often. She is liberated from worrying about calories, weight or clogged arteries. At this point she can have whatever she wants.

The day has progressed, she thinks. The sun has moved, the light has moved. She has taken meds. Possibly something has changed. Certainly her system has calmed. There is a stack of library books to go back to the library. She has read an anthology called *More Stories We Tell*, and she was irritated by Alice Munro, who keeps, to her mind anyhow, writing the same story over and over. She has made a note for Helen to be on the lookout for several new authors whose books she would like to send to her mother. She can see from her open chequebook that she has sent money to David Suzuki. She has signed a petition, and now the phone rings. She doesn't move, lets the machine pick up, and of course it is her mother. She goes on about her sister in California, the new house her son bought her in Alameda, or some suburb, how cold it is in Terrace, where she moved recently to be near Annie. She will go on at length and say nothing, but what Therese can hear throughout is the desire for forgiveness, the desire to be let off the hook. She would let her off the hook if she could. She has tried, but there is a refusal to be let off the hook. As if she enjoys the dangling. Has always enjoyed it.

When Therese had gotten out to her mother's before their final drama began, her mother's pulse was so low the ambulance attendants couldn't find it. She was close to death, the doctor said later, after they had stabilized her. She is lucky you arrived when you did, the medic said. Adel had not adjusted to life without Jean. Therese found herself living in her mother's trailer, dealing with various crazy neighbours, and doctors, but she did advocate for her mother. She organized her medications. Made charts. Cleaned. She stayed even after Adel was strong enough to come home. And, evidently, she stayed too long.

Does it faze her yet? Death, her long-time companion? When she saw Marilyn and Dave go over the rail she remembered calmly placing the glass of Coke on a coaster before running down the stairs. Impossible to take the elevator, even the three flights of stairs seemed ridiculous: the human mind is surely meant to teleport. As she ran, she felt herself falling head over heels through air. By the time she was down and out to the front of the building, blood was pooling under Marilyn's head. Dave had landed on her and he was unconscious still. A soccer team had come across the field, several children on tricycles stood gaping. Marilyn was a big woman. Dave thin and reedy. A woman appeared from nowhere and was holding Marilyn's head. There was blood coming out of her mouth. Therese knew not to move the head and yelled at her to stop but she already had Marilyn's chin up. Dave came to then and looked at her like a very lost, very small boy. He said something, Therese can't recall what, but his face when he realized he was on Marilyn, that he had squashed her – that was a look she would never forget. Had they been drinking, the police asked later. Had they been fighting? Therese stayed with the children, a boy and a girl, blond, preschool. Shortly after, Dave moved away.

Therese recalled them all on the landing in the Winnipeg house, straining to hear what was being said below. When death comes into your childhood, you remember strange details. You remember your siblings there: Annie on her toes, peering over, Jerry and Bjarne against the wall, tensed, as if they were holding it up, Guddy with her feet tucked into her pyjamas. The two policemen seemed to expand the hallway below, the stairs flexed like lungs. She thought she could see footprints from where she and Bjarne had climbed up the wall, ready to drop down on the cousins who sometimes babysat on bingo nights. Annie looked like a pane of cracked glass.

Her brother lasted two nights in a coma before dying, the morning of Bjarne's birthday, which, along with hers, being the same day as Joe's, would become an unbirthday, to be uncelebrated along with unChristmas and unEaster and unHalloween, which were all terrible reminders of something lost.

And then that horrible *My baby, my baby* that rang through the house week after week after week. And all these years later, that note, lingering in her voice still. Poor Adel, as if the loss happened only to her.

'I love you,' her mother says finally, an exaggerated pout followed by a long pause. She has learned how long she can pause for effect before the machine cuts her off. 'I am not perfect, but I love you.'

She knows her mother loves her. Or believes she loves her. Of course she knows. It seems unbelievable to her that she does, but she does. Guddy sent her an essay by bell hooks illuminating the insane behaviours we accept as evidence of familial love.

She has written several drafts of letters to her mother, but none of them has been completed or sent. It is too late for them, too late for smoothing over. She tried. They both tried. Now there is only acceptance.

In the realm of illness, it is unfair for the ill, first of all, to be ill, and second to have to deal with everyone else's experience of their illness. They have all, even Guddy, disappointed her.

Sledgehammers, garbage trucks, delivery vans backing up, men breaking up pavement to lay pipes and repave once more, car alarms, tires skidding, and below it all the perky insistence of the black-capped chickadee, and what sounds like the three baleful notes of the white-throated sparrow: this last isn't what wakes her, but it is what saves her mood for the day. She knows that Pema would say *Let the noise flow through you, don't let it stick.* Fuck Pema. Pema doesn't have cancer. She hasn't been popping OxyContin, nor as far as Therese is aware, does her liver resemble a lace doily.

It is the first day in weeks she is without pain on her right side. There are messages from several old friends whom she doesn't feel like talking to just now. They want to hear she is fine. She is a constant reminder of the body's fragility and she is sick of it. She doesn't want to be anyone's wake-up call. Fuck you. It's boring; of course she gets snappy. She sees it in their faces when they run into her. She's still alive, their surprise says. Even the soccer team, after all those years. I thought we had said goodbye, they think, I already gave at the fundraiser, they think. Well, that's the problem with beating the odds: guilt for doing well. Not that she feels the least bit guilty. She is more likely to feel irritated, to feel hurt by the looks, and she refuses to put them at ease. They should be putting her at ease.

On the other hand, yes, they have been good friends. Very good friends. She has been blessed with good friends who visit (though not often enough, lately), who have helped her through many moves, many crises, fundraising on her behalf – making a perfect summer at Halfmoon Bay possible. Together they had huge cookouts. She grew flowers and filmed them all summer. The bees that came to the cone-flower, the poppies with legs like dancers, the inchworm and violet, the scarlet runner beans, the pileated woodpecker. Her beautiful, irritating friends made all of that possible. She would kiss each of them on the tips of their noses like tiny hummingbirds.

But it doesn't stop the strangeness – the gulf between the living and the dying. She is always aware of her death. It is

172

just underfoot, just around the corner. She has no future, whereas everyone around her is blissfully imagining his or hers; conscious or not, it guides them, makes possible their every move. They also might not have a future, but they aren't thinking that.

She has been reading about the Canadian soldiers who were involved in the atomic bomb tests in the Arctic. They were in trenches when it went off. They were there to see how effective the trenches could be in the face of the bomb. 'You heard a click and there was this flash of light so intense I could see the bones in my arm,' a soldier said.

When they gave her chemo – against her wishes they gave her chemo – they told her that one drop would burn a hole through her skin. *Why are you putting this into my body then? Why are you radiating and chemicalling my body?*

Is she being fair? Perhaps this isn't time for fair. There are times for fairness, and then there are times for anger.

Today she feels like she is in a Bill Viola film, light buckling like thick, concave rounds of construction paper above her as she slowly sinks down through a frigid body of water, her hands trailing bubbles, completely unaware that she is not safe. It doesn't feel unsafe. It feels miraculous, the texture of the water on her skin, moving through her hair, like the first time they went to Winnipeg Beach. The sun was shining. It was so warm that solid things loosened and seemed to float away from themselves. Therese felt buoyant too, her limbs with ideas of their own, and though she doubts she had ever seen a lake before that day, she ran the length of the pier and continued right off the end into the water. The cold of it was a blissful shock, but then the depth. She had somehow expected to float. Which she didn't. Then she thought she might find a bottom. But no, she kept sinking until she opened her eyes and saw the pylons, thick and mossy. She looked up and there was her light. So far away and undulating, as if it were crackling and shooting in vertical rays. She crawled toward it, breaking into air. But to her surprise there was no stepping out. Down she went again. This time she began to panic and flail, to take in water, to feel the fluidness of it, the absolute instability of her body in this new environment, the boundaries breaking down, the outside coming in. The texture seemed to have changed instantly and now all was cold, mysterious, black. She scrambled for the surface, broke through to light, and again could not get out. She could see her mother on the pier, waving her arms, screaming for help. Adel never could swim, was terrified of water. Therese went down again, and again panicked, kicked, flailed to remain in the air, and then suddenly Adel was there beside her, red polka-dot dress floating up around them. She was flailing too, but she had Therese in her arms, and Therese knew she was safe; even though neither of them could swim, her mother would not let her go. Finally someone found a life ring and tossed it to them. Her mother grabbed it and they were hauled to shore.

In the beginning there was light, and in moving toward that, story. Whatever else matters little … well, aside from the inevitable fact of her illness holding her back. Though now she has to ask herself whether or not this is pain speaking – the Prednisone, which has given her so much freedom these past few years, has suddenly flared out. The mask has dropped. She is a beached whale, bloated and throbbing. They warned her this would happen. The pain is real: psychic as well as physical. And there is no recovering.

What does any of this have to do with Guddy? Therese reserves a particular anger for her: didn't she walk away from Therese's suffering? And couldn't they have been closer? They have so much in common and yet it always feels one-way with Guddy. And worse, Therese suspects it is a sense of guilt that keeps them in contact. When Guddy was just a teenager, she got mad and wrote a note to Therese saying that she was her hero, she loved her, but if they weren't sisters they wouldn't be friends. It wasn't easy to be her sister, Guddy wrote, *you have to understand.*

Understand what? That she isn't reliable? That she isn't going to stick around? Didn't she fly out of the cage and then do her the disservice of constantly, half-heartedly looking back? Banging her way back into the cage. Reminding Therese of the cage. Couldn't she have released them both instead?

Therese had her respect once, and lost it. Therese had been her hero, and lost it. Dropped like a brick from the sky after some slight indiscretion that she can't recall. She is not blind: Therese knows that the monthly phone call is now just to assuage guilt. Does she mind that Guddy isn't coming for the holidays? She'd best not mind, considering she hasn't bothered to come home for the holidays in half a decade and when she did it wasn't all that pleasant. So, does Therese mind that her sister is taking care of herself first?

It's her choice. Guilt is the price of surviving, she knows that. Guddy knows that. Why must she constantly relieve her of it?

Why can't she simply say: I hate Guddy. I won't forgive her. Why is it so difficult to be clear, to explain the relationship of one conflict to another, how one decision leads to another. *My childhood caused me cancer*, she could say, and offer an image of a pre–Rachel Carson moment that saw herself and her siblings running after a truck spraying DDT over the lawns to fight the persistent mosquito problem. My mother oppressed me, the church filled with me with self-loathing, I wasted years of my life trying *not* to be gay: any of these statements are ludicrous; she can see that, though it doesn't stop her from feeling them, from feeling generally pissed off at the world.

Perhaps her own ravaging curiosity made life difficult for her mother, whom she has a twinge of compassion for now, for both of them, for their exhausting years of fighting, of harsh words. Not enough to pick up the phone, or even answer the erratically timed calls. Or perhaps the compassion for herself cancels out the compassion for her mother. Self-defence, she would argue in a court of law: it was her or me, and I chose me.

Suffice to say that they are at odds. Her mother is narcissistic, bombastic, histrionic, mean and, worse, incapable of learning. At this point, Therese has no more energy to waste on anyone or anything that isn't either giving her pleasure or easing her pain, unless it is in some way benefitting the world at large; she can suffer for that.

But she won't suffer for the past. Not any longer. The past cuts people off from the present, from the ability to react to it with any force, that she's sure of. How many times had her father come in from his workshop to verify, in passing, some fact from a story set in 1957 that her mother was telling, shaking his head, *Yes, woman, that is a fact, woman.* How many times had he begged her mother, pleaded with her to give up the past, and how many times had he argued that without a sense of the past they were doomed?

She is beginning to doubt that we ever leave childhood … to think the past is a narcotic.

Therese's autobiography will not detail squabbles, harsh words, abuses; no, her autobiography will be multiple screens on which long swaths of light will be cast ... not sublime but euphoric half-shells; oblique ferns; moss-covered stones; water-filled peach pits; inchworms teetering like Slinkys on giant leaves; silken dewy cocoons; the trail behind her cabin at Halfmoon Bay with its fawning salal; burning cedar; wood grain; ant trails; ant hills; clouds moving at all speeds, shot from up above, from Cypress, or from the bow of a boat looking up, up, contrails bursting into flocks of starlings; wind in the firs building into forest fires, walls of flames inching down mountainsides; the nose of a deer; the paw of a bear rooting for grubs; a constant unravelling of images. No words. Not one.

She wakes from a dream in which she is at home – her mother's home, so more a nightmare, but wait, it isn't quite her mother's home, it's bigger, more spacious, maybe the version of her mother that exists underneath the damaged shell of the mother that she knows. She is leaving, taking her own structure with her because suddenly she is aware that she has, is, a structure of her own. That is to say, she is firm. She tells her mother this. She is independent. Mobile. A composite of organic and inorganic materials. She pulses with life, glows. Is glass and bone, amphibious, self-generating. My God, she is a wonder!

At first her mother is reluctant to let her go, but finally agrees to let her leave. This is when Therese realizes she is not a person, her mother, she is a kind of material, like plaster, covering the insides of the walls. Therese tries to run, to manoeuvre her way out, but her huge house within the house grows as she moves. She considers the hallway and foyer a possible impasse, but when she approaches them she realizes her house truly is mobile, and collapsible, and she is very relieved not to have to bump against her mother.

Her final gaze around the room seems to give her mother a fresh coat of paint, white and luminous. You can let go, she tells her mother. You can.

She feels like a whale navigating icebergs, or Orlando on waking as a woman, traversing the corridor in white, a kite amongst the white drapery, furniture and former lovers under wraps.

I have cancer, she says to Orlando as she skates past. They are on the Thames now, and it is frozen. *I have had it for most of my adult life*, she tells him/her, casually managing perfect circles. *I live with and defy it. I don't meditate on it, don't give it any of my light, my precious light: I move against it. I say fuck it!* She goes on even as it crawls and re-forms itself from one side of her body to the other. Never mind, she has defied convention. Defied treatment. Watched as friends and family are diagnosed, treated (or mistreated, in her opinion) and die. She is still here, though. She is going on her twentieth year with it; she has outlived all of her friends with AIDS and HIV. She has a scar on her right breast, she has scars under her arms, she has a broken heart, but she is here, she awaits the light. Whether or not Orlando has heard she can't tell, they are both skating around a firepit and when she realizes that she is without a muffler and should be cold, the scene ends abruptly.

She squeezes through an opening and finds herself in a field, in a windstorm. Guddy is there, as well as several horses, nervously pacing back and forth, snorting, and in the process, squishing her and Guddy against the sides of the corral, for suddenly they are in one, a corral, or a feedlot, and there are more horses than space to move. She keeps thinking hamburger, which is not the right outcome for horses, or houses, but it is where her mind goes. The meat grinder at the corner store in her youth where she stared up at the strings of hamburger pouring out as Lynn, the shopkeeper, ground. She is aware of how much she wants to be with

Guddy now. How much she loves her, but she won't admit it. Why should she? Guddy has made her life difficult. She remains so distanced. They pace, the horses between them, until there is nowhere to move, at which point Therese sets them free with a wink.

That is how it's done, she tells Guddy. Their dark, sinewy, rippling muscles tear into sky.

The dream continues but she can't remember the rest. She wakes feeling full, but in pain, which means she won't eat again today.

Never mind, she has had her share. She has eaten well.

She is thinking of Adel's attempts to mate her. To set her up with various men she thought might take her off her hands. What makes a mother engage in such behaviour she'll never know, but the final straw came in the small town of Nakusp, when she forced her to go out with Rick. There was something creepy about him, of course there was, the way he never looked anyone in the eye, and later she found out that Guddy had her own story of Rick to tell and she had a flash of guilt, just a splash of guilt at abandoning her sister to that. But how was she to know? Wasn't her main concern, at fifteen, her own survival? Surely that is fair? She had gone out on the date, neither of them talking, and he dropping her home untouched and early (little did they know she was already too old for him) but entirely disturbed. Feeling entirely unsafe. She had spent the date planning her escape, and that night, after they were all asleep, she took forty dollars from Adel's purse, a kitchen knife, her father's camera and the crucifix, which she left smashed outside the motel room door.

There was no traffic in the middle of the night, so she walked along the road, cold but not snowy, dark but not frightening, the shape of the mountains, and the air, as if she were the first to breathe it, was cool and fresh. Just as the sun was coming up a man in a bread truck picked her up (he wasn't supposed to have riders, he said, but why was she out in the middle of nowhere?) and drove her to Revelstoke. He bought her breakfast at a truck stop, where he ran into a friend heading south to Vancouver, and so she had a safe, uneventful trip. Ironically much less eventful than almost any trip she had been dragged on with Adel.

They were both good men and each gave her forty dollars to add to the forty she stole from Adel's purse, so she had emergency funds. It wasn't such a long journey, not that first night, but it was the start of something much longer, much more difficult. Impossible really, leaving Adel behind. Leaving childhood behind.

My childhood kicking cans in alleys. My childhood full of song. My childhood crickets, flying squirrels, dew worms, fields of cows. How does she get that down on film? She doesn't. Instead she looks out. She looks outside the constant reels of childhood. On Mayne Island the butterflies circled purple loosestrife. She filmed ladybugs fucking in the early morning; even tumbling through lavender they somehow remained joined. She looked and she looked and she looked, at the sea urchins' gentle reach, at the starfishes' slow progress, at the waves, at the sun abstracting on surfaces, at the cars with their attitudes, the chromes, the plastic with its curves, the movement of a kite, the wing of bird, the earthworm's surprise at air, the ant with its larvae, the snake shedding its skin, the moth's determination, the robin's cocked ear, the blooming of poppies, the air, the air, the air, rough as cedar on her face, the bobbing freighters, the crows overhead, the crows calling and calling with some urgency, with some specific urgency in mind.

She wakes and Helen is there at her side. 'What's happening?'

'You were sleeping,' Helen says. 'You were dreaming. Very busily. Your feet. Were you cycling?'

'Around the seawall. With Lyle, I think.'

'It's a good day for cycling. You can see the Sisters.'

'I don't feel myself,' Therese says, not quite understanding what she wants to say. Then very clearly: 'I don't think this body is serving any purpose.'

Helen pulls the blanket up around her and irritated, Therese, with some exaggeration, loosens it again. She quickly regrets her snap and then the regret it makes her feel. It is a long line of reprimand and self-negation, and she is weary of it.

'It's nice that you're here,' she says.

'Of course I'm here.'

Helen's confidence grates, but she decides to let it go and surprisingly it vanishes and she thinks of the shore, walking on Third Beach, filming the tide, the screech of gulls, of cyclists and babies. 'Do you think you have left your childhood?'

'What do you mean?'

'I mean do you have it with you? Now? Or is it just memory?'

'Maybe it always was memory? Maybe we only imbue it with feeling after the fact.'

Nonsense, she is thinking. There are the hard facts of childhood. Those with, those without, those who win, those who are given centre stage and those assigned parts of background noise, walk-ons, all the way down to audience, and then the sweepers who don't even get to witness life ... She could include the bones of the poor who are pulverized as fertilizer at the altar of market, but she stops short of that because at the moment it rings too true. Everything, in fact, suddenly rings too true.

'Maybe it's just an illusion,' Helen says, but she doesn't want to hear Helen at the moment. She is thinking of the intrusions, the interruptions ... there was no single event, they were all walking the gauntlet of childhood with its sharp surfaces.

Is that what memory is? A catalogue of event? Of trauma? No wonder she destroyed her journals. Who wants to know about one childhood among many? And a flawed one at that. Listen, she thinks, flaws are only interesting when they are overcome. The one-armed tennis star, the blind pianist, the poverty-stricken rock star, the mentally challenged soprano; her survival is not enough to make her interesting. Doesn't everyone want their pain to be relevant? To be interesting? Perhaps she should have trotted out all her wounds in her art.

She has, by her bed, an article from the *Globe and Mail* tracing the struggle families encounter after the loss of a child. She could not contain herself as she read. She began to make notes in the margins: Juicy Fruit. The day her brother Joe died he had offered her a piece of Juicy Fruit gum. She was mad at him because he had hit her. Take the gum, he said, as if it made everything better. I don't want anything from you, she said. I wish you were dead. He made her count to ten before she ran away. Now she realizes he was worried because he had hit her so hard her head banged against the pavement. Maybe he was in as much pain as she was. Maybe she had a lump on her head. The ones with physical symptoms are lucky, Guddy told her, people can see the pain. She had disagreed with Guddy, but now she sees what she means.

What had happened to Joe to make him so angry that day? She can't remember. All she remembers is running away, and then turning to see him disappear into the cemetery where they played hide-and-seek, and Therese yelling after him then, over and over again, *I wish you were dead.*

Ach, she thinks. Looking back. Looking forward. She would rather be looking through a lens. The digital world is so much more beautiful than real life. We are only shadows of our childhoods in any case. She could train her camera on the water's surface, how changeable it is, its moods no less benign than humans. Walking the seawall could cure her of anything; if only she could get to Third Beach, where she hasn't been in weeks. She tries to remember the last time she was there. She would go now, when the light is golden, and she would stand near the red-and-white lifeboat and watch the sun descend.

But that doesn't give you an idea of what she is seeing: the bands of light, blue, bluer, blue with a hint of pink, blue with a hint of mauve nestling there between the tip of West Vancouver and the freighter that looks to be just due north of Kitsilano but is probably not. The various cloud formations, now white puffs of cotton, now thin and rippled like a sea floor, now bruised blue with greyer bits upright and jagged as Banff shale. And the boats, three or six or nine of them out there slowly rotating on their anchors. She has been up close to them, photographed the hulls, marked like the skin of elephants. They are so much bigger than one can imagine from shore. They are part of the dark herd and likely contain uranium, or toxins that will devastate her bay, but she welcomes them nonetheless for there is so much that is good about the future, so much that excites her even as the virtual world pulls, and she wants to say *yes*.

Not that she is ready for the virtual world entirely. She has spent hours plugged into Halo, but that is too passive still. What she wants to be is a conduit. She wants her nerve ends to caress the earth's surface as democratically and erotically as the lowly garden slug, but she also wants to screen what she sees with her own eyes. She wants to be a splash of red on a crisp blade of grass, and a pixel fitting into the folds of a curtain. All of this she thinks of as colour gliding over surface, textures melting together like thick, shallow rapids, the glint of stone through water, wood through fire, humans through technology's scrim. If she could spend eternity doing anything, this would be it: a lens on the moment, the unfurling.

But she is not – at least not yet – a lens, or a fir tree, or light, or air, and suddenly she is a body. She is a body in pain. The pain is much more than she can bear. She considers trying to paint the pain but it comes out black, as though she has left the lens cap on. Perhaps the morphine is not dripping. Perhaps Helen has for some reason unplugged it. She can hear Helen breathing beside her. Small, direct breaths, quick, mindful movements, each one a tiny meditation, a validation. She has done well finding her. They had good years together and still she is her most loyal friend. There are other noises too, people in a hallway, a cart passing, strange voices. No drain spout, no Guillaume as she had thought. Earlier someone, perhaps Susan, came by but she made everyone promise not to let anyone in. This comes to her very clearly now. Only Helen, and Guddy, who is on her way, can see her. She has known this, and not, and something in her begins to panic, the something that knows why Guddy is coming. She opens her eyes, turns. Helen squeezes her hand in return.

'Am I dying?'

Helen's face flashes through a series of emotions, but she doesn't flinch. 'Soon,' she says. 'You are probably dying soon.'

'Oh,' she says, 'I had no idea.'

'How are you feeling?'

'I am in a lot of pain. I don't think I can take any more pain.'

'No, you don't have to.'

She is suddenly aware of another presence in the room. The nurse, a tall man in white with grey hair and a face that looks like a composite of all the lovely men she has known in her life stands at the foot of her bed.

'I have a shot for you, Therese.'

'Thank you,' she says.

'She's in a lot of pain,' Helen says, and he nods.

'I don't think I can take any more,' she says, feeling suddenly like a very bad girl, a girl who has not, will not, withstand what life has to offer. She is going down, but this time she can't control the tears and doesn't bother to try, and to her surprise the tears do not come out, but rather, somehow, she senses them falling inside her. Down her throat, along her ribs, a tickling salty trail.

'You don't need to take any more, the nurse says.'

Helen leans in, touches her cheek. 'You might not wake up again, Therese.'

'I know,' she says. 'I know.' She hadn't wanted it to be like this. She wanted it to be at home. Perhaps this is still possible, but not while she is in so much pain. The nurse moves quickly. She follows the patch of light on her knuckle, up across Helen's face, and into the wall where she has drawings from the children in her life, flowers on the sill, facing out to the sentinel mountains of her city, and she thinks maybe, beyond everything, the city has been the love of her life. This city, the seawall, the bridges, the buildings old and new, the market, the boats, the mountains, so in need of protection. She is cold suddenly and feels tiny wings unfolding and stretching. Silly, she thinks, all these years with wings and she didn't use them. Why had she not thought to use them? And surely now she is crushing them. 'Am I crushing my wings?'

'No, you're fine.'

Oh, she thinks, I'm fine.

'I love you,' Helen says.

'I know,' Therese says. Or does she? Has she just thought this? Has she told Helen she loves her too? The light hasn't abandoned her quite yet but it is descending. She is descending into something. She is thinking about this when she hears Guddy come into the room. She is calm, but she knows her sister: it's a surface calm. She stands in the doorway with Helen, who is patient, non-judging. She walks across the room, across the light, which Therese senses. Guddy wouldn't block her light, she knows that much. Guddy is not deliberately difficult. Therese is hoping she will settle in. Will sit and let her get back to the business of aligning her body with the light. She has no idea where this knowledge comes from but she is relieved to have it. Death is busy, she thinks, who knew?

Guddy sits, finally, after flitting about the room. They both sink into themselves. Tibia lengths of muscle, vessels, flaccid but pumping slowly. Air moves across her and she feels it pass out of her, which soothes. It's always moving, she thinks, and this seems like huge news. Her knees soften, her feet fall to the side: a burst of light reaches her cheek and all of her energy gathers there, the mole and lines, the lashes, soaking it in. She twitches and Guddy stands. This isn't about you, she wants to say to her sister who thinks everything is about her, and not only the good, but she can't. She can't speak at all and thinks for a minute that she doesn't miss speech. What a bother it has been – searching for the right tone, not the word, words are a little easier, it is tone that eludes her, tone that makes her life difficult. This thought sends her into a panic because she never did like the word *no*, the words *cannot* or *never again* ... and there is twitching throughout her, involuntary twitching, which again makes Guddy stir and she leaves the room.

The feeling of her body loosening is a good thing and she wants to concentrate on that. As much as she has wanted to wring out every embodied moment, she knows that the body is not really her. Underneath all this illness and pain is her true self and she has a sense she might finally see what that is. She tries to remember that, to hold on to it as her body begins to shudder through the injection. Her true self might be nothing more than air. O kidneys, she thinks, O liver, O heart, O internal organs … you have held on through all of this. You have remained intact. You are wonderful. And then her mother appears with her arms out. No, she thinks. No, not that. And she panics. I don't want her here, not now. I don't want to think of her. Or see her. She has no right to invade this space.

She is thinking of a dream she has had variations of her entire life. She is being chased by something very dark, very dangerous. She goes to a door – it is a familiar door, Annie's, or perhaps it is one of the many houses of her childhood. She is both excited and frightened. She is hoping she will be soothed. There is some anticipation on her part. She knocks and it is her mother who answers. She opens the door and before she can say anything she reaches out and guts Therese with a twelve-inch curved blade. She starts at the bottom of her belly and very calmly rips her open to her neck. At least she always thought it was her mother cutting her; now she thinks perhaps it is the other way around. How is that possible?

Who is holding on to whom here? Who keeps the dream alive?

She is reminded of a series of portraits she did in art school. While developing the negatives the water went from sixty-eight degrees to boiling, which made the emulsion melt, and when she realized this she splashed cold water in, and in doing so froze the processing so that the portraits looked as though her body was being eaten away from belly to breast. She destroyed these images, along with most – nearly all – of her art, in the mid-to-late phase of her third diagnosis, when it seemed she had nothing to live for.

She had regretted it almost immediately. So much seeing and yet not a trace left behind.

Guddy comes in again. Depression is more deadly than cancer, she wants to tell her, don't let yourself go there, and forgive me for my long stay.

She regrets destroying everything. She regrets lost time. It wasn't a prefiguring of her disease; it was how she saw herself. It was never her mother who wanted to slice her open. It was always herself. Always wanting to slice away this thick, dark, oppressive skin that pulled her around, that had a life of its own. She is trying hard to hold on to the train of thought. She wants to make sure Guddy hears this. But Guddy is not hearing anything. She says something about Philadelphia, she says something about a new job, and Therese thinks of overripe fruit, or the rollercoaster at the PNE, a gang of her friends stealing the prize-winning cheese. Guddy is telling her about her life. 'So you'll know where I am,' she says. But Therese simply sees colours moving across a screen, faces morphing from one to another, which reminds her of a series of Polaroids from the early eighties. She had taken a portrait of each of her friends. So many faces lining the walls, so many beautiful, open faces. She liked to manipulate the background. She would put them in the toaster to loosen the chemicals and with the nub of a pencil or the tip of a paintbrush she could redraw the lines, making it new, and new again. But then the colours start to bleed and the tickle in her chest pulls at her, as if she has a string on the inside.

Then she sees Guddy standing on a horse, agile as a ballet dancer, her hands in the air, urging her to come. She is so delighted she feels a rush of adrenaline and the muscle under her own feet and they are both riding down Robson Street, the old Robson Street, with the Mutual Café, and the German diners. They are both filled with joy, spurts of pure joy. It is rush hour but there are no cars, there is no anger, only the knots of emotion hanging in the air like those hooks hanging from gymnasium roofs for lengths of rope to climb. There is nothing to do but grab one, and then another. There is simply being, a timeless, deep now, and they are in it, swinging over the city like circus performers.

She isn't crying, but there is water inside her, and she tries to cough it up. Guddy stops, turns on her horse. She can't stop coughing. She slips down; her thighs warm on the flanks, gripping the mane. Why don't humans have manes, she wonders. It would be so much more convenient to grip each other like this.

And then she realizes that of course we don't hold on. We can't. She must let go of each bone, each muscle, each organ, cell, molecule, memory, thought, desire – lightening, lightening – and when the light comes, when she sees it, she is filled with coolness, her body gives way, her bones soften, her mind lightens. She will not wait for goodbyes, doesn't even look back at the container that held her, that caused her so much pain and pleasure and pain. She is up and out and over the city, bolting through one or two houses, where she feels a tug, quick and sleek, a flash, and she is free, body undulating, ribbons and tails in the air.

Her eyes scan the children, all of them in their own way beautiful. Her eyes move up and down the rows, the various coifs, the mismatched outfits, the pinking lips, the shoulders pinched. Some children are taller. They are bunched in the centre of the top row. They may or may not be standing on benches (hardwood benches, highly varnished, solid tributes to childhoods capable of circling basketball games). Some of the children have been fussed over. Some of the children wear crisp outfits. Some of them have neat hair, freshly trimmed. Some have tumbled out of bed, have struggled out of nightmares. Some have walked across war zones, have scavenged food, have watched their parents die, and kept walking. They are all in the same photo, elbow to elbow; childhood flattens them into a single expression, fits them in a single frame.

Child abandoned in alley behind casino. Child left on hospital steps. Child found in restroom in Walmart. Three children left to freeze. Children found in lining of truck. Children sold into sex trade. Child survives by living with wolves. Children protest nuclear arms, rally for their future.

How random the state of childhood, how the value of a childhood fluctuates.

So many childhoods to account for and yet we come back again and again to our own. To the nut of our own experience, the exactitude of it, the supreme making of our lives charted out in those early breaths, those first brushes with danger, the revelations ... We are sucked back into the intensity of the moment, the vista of mother. This childhood, this mother's humming a soft weave, this mother's voice a cool sheet on a warm afternoon. Childhood leaps and frolics, is slapped down and stunned.

The fact that even after her mother has been cruel,
even after she has abandoned her, or smacked her across
the face sharply in public, her gaze can soothe, because
childhood is forgiving even if startling. She is as startled
by her behaviour as you are. You stare across the gulf of
impropriety, shaken. You turn your head at the check-
out counter, you watch the mother drag the child
through the aisles and shake your head.

The little girl at the Y stares at her, one hand
stretched out to the locker, mildly curious. When a child
stares out who stares back? Who meets the gaze of a two-
year-old, or a four-year-old? Seen now, suddenly on the
street, seen, really seen by someone, it is rarely the ones
who should see.

Now you will say she is this or that. Now she is still
a child, or she holds her hand out, or reaches up. Now
her legs muscle and, indeed, the length of the books she
attacks grows. And now she is busy collecting baseball
cards and bottle caps, hoping for LPs or trips to Disney-
land. Mark the text here, turn a corner of the page,
for now she is sweetening. Somewhere someone is climb-
ing the Empire State Building with no regard whatever
for childhood.

And yet we all yearn for childhood, revel in our own
versions of it. The dappled clouds, the scent of our
father's labour, our mother's decadence, our siblings'
discoveries, intellectual, sexual, our childhood in the
woods, stretched out in a field of fireweed or lady ferns,
our childhood in malls, pining. Wherever it is or was we
pine for it. In childhood, time is resplendent. Time is
pornographic. It lingers on warm afternoons, an
extended, innocent arousal, and stretching out in what-
ever space it is given. You might be looking death in the
face, but there are always moments: the sun beats

down, you have a reprieve, you move into a tract of woods (there are always woods here on the fringe of childhood, small strips awaiting development), the woods are steaming with themselves, you trace the mark your father's machinery makes, nudging the wilderness, progress unwinding, trees falling, bear and caribou conversing like women, expectant, still, thinking there must be some trick in it all, but no, they are not taken into account, like the Natives they are resources, guides, and once they are inducted into museums, they are a pleasant aside.

There is a trick to the inside-out of things. Progress, like sorting laundry after an extended vacation, how the socks are righted, tucked neatly; everyone enjoys the moment of replenishment. And childhood replenishes as much as it drains. Childhood hardens moments and brands them on your skin, in your mind, small bumps of consciousness that worry. Childhood, beloved, delicate, powdered, we flit in it, blind and surprising as butterflies; we hurl ourselves over treetops searching for colour, light, the erotics of stamen and pistil, the force driving us through.

And then it is gone, underground, pale under the skin: tiny bruises, or orchid blossoms burned into the flesh, visible in flashes of joy or rage. Momentary spurts of it. She has not walked away from her childhood, she realizes, she has walked toward it. There she is on the big rock at the river, a skipping rope in hand. There he is on the beach with his ruined castle. There she is having taken first prize in the relay race. There he is having skinned his knees and up again, onto his older brother's bike. There she is figuring out long division, the best method of skinning a rabbit. There he is uncomfortable with even the slightest hint of softness.

We plant our childhoods like flags. We insist on them. We say: this geography, this materiality, these emotional landmines, this is who I am. We insist on them because without them we are nothing.

ACKNOWLEDGEMENTS

An excerpt from an early draft of this novel, translated by Florence Trocmé, appeared in *Siècle 21*, out of Paris, France, in 2006. Thanks to Marilyn Hacker for the invitation. I would like to thank the Canada Council for the Arts, the Banff Centre for the Arts, the Markin Flanagan Writer-in-Residence program at the University of Calgary, and Jackie Flanagan, for time and support in writing this novel. Greg Hollingshead and Marilyn Bowering gave early feedback. Alana Wilcox once again proves to have the best eye ever. Danielle Bobker, as always.

ABOUT THE AUTHOR

Sina Queyras's last collection of poetry, *Expressway*, was nominated for a Governor General's Award and won Gold at the National Magazine Awards. Her previous collection, *Lemon Hound*, won a Lambda Award and the Pat Lowther Award. She has taught creative writing at Rutgers and Concordia University in Montreal, where she lives.

Typeset in Walbaum and Barrett
Printed and bound at the Coach House on bpNichol Lane, 2011

Edited and designed by Alana Wilcox
Cover design by Ingrid Paulson
Author photo by Danielle Bobker

Coach House Books
80 bpNichol Lane
Toronto ON M5S 3J4

416 979 2217
800 367 6360

mail@chbooks.com
www.chbooks.com